The Girl with a Broken Heart

Based on a True Story

The Girl with a Broken Heart

Based on a True Story

Ramos Talaya

For more info:

www.ramostalaya.com

www.facebook.com/psRamosTalaya

www.twitter.com/RamosTalaya

www.youtube.com/user/RamosTalaya

www.amazon.com/author/ramostalaya

www.linkedin.com/RamosTalaya

instagram.com/ramos_talaya/

To order additional copies of this book, please contact:

Sagacity Media, **Call/WhatsApp**: 083 344 7096 **Email**: brxpta@gmail.com

CONTENTS

Dedicated to all rape and abuse victims.

You are not alone.

CHAPTER ONE

I t was her first time; it was marvellous, but it tasted bitter in the end.

She broke a promise in exchange for another promise.

It was a risky transaction, like money in the hands of an addicted gambler.

The deed was irreversible. The promise was as sure as one could be assured of winning the lottery.

Yet she forged ahead regardless, put her heart and body on the table, crossing her fingers, hoping the promise would be fulfilled. But she was left to pick up the pieces of her shattered heart, alone. And this is how it all began…

Bonelwa, a twenty-one-year-old young woman with an ultra-conservative upbringing, was from a small town in the Eastern Cape. She had always dreamed of having a perfect life; a successful career in journalism, a tall, dark, handsome, loving and rich husband, and two children—a boy and a girl.

Bonelwa was very beautiful in appearance and form. She was short and had lovely brown eyes, long dark hair, and a friendly personality.

After graduating from high school, Bonelwa and her best friend Zuki applied for admission at the University of Cape Town.

It was a happy day when they both received their admission letters, notifying them that they had been accepted at the University.

In her second year at the University, she met Tau, a senior in his last year. It was love at first sight for both of them, at least it seemed so at the time. After dating for six months, Bonelwa decided to give Tau the gift of her virginity at the ripe age of twenty-one!

Tau was delighted, and impressed at the same time, that Bonelwa was still a virgin.

It was on a Valentine's Day, when he gently deflowered Bonelwa.

He held and gently kissed Bonelwa through the night until the early hours of the morning, constantly reassuring her of his love for her when he realized that she seemed unsure if she had done the right thing, or if she should have waited for the man that would marry her. Though Tau ticked all the right boxes on her secret list, she wondered silently through the night if she would later regret her decision to give Tau her virginity.

Tau's gentleness and reassurance of his love for her put her fears at ease and helped her to relax in his strong arms wrapped around her.

As they continued to date, their love for each other grew stronger and stronger. So strong were Bonelwa's feelings toward Tau that she could no longer contain her big secret, so she decided to tell Zuki all about it.

Zuki was surprised, and envious at the same time, that Bonelwa was still a virgin at the age of twenty-one. Zuki had lost her virginity at the age of sixteen. Bonelwa wanted to tell Zuki many times that she was still a virgin, but she couldn't bring herself to reveal her virginity. She was ashamed, and feared the ridicule and mockery of her peers, so she decided to conceal it…until now.

The more Bonelwa talked about her first time with Tau, the more details Zuki wanted—and the more details she gave Zuki, the more Zuki wanted to experience it herself.

The opportune time came on summer holiday when Bonelwa decided to visit her family in Eastern Cape. Tau had his final examination scheduled for after the holidays, so he decided to stay on campus to study and prepare for his final exams.

One Friday night after midnight, as she returned from the club more than a bit tipsy, Zuki decided to visit the other side of the campus and knock on Tau's door. Surprised by her way past hours visit, Tau reluctantly let her in into his room, taking into consideration that she was Bonelwa's best friend. It didn't take long for Tau to realize that Zuki was drunk. Emboldened by the alcohol, Zuki wasted no time in letting Tau know the reason for her late night visit.

"Tau, I've heard it all and I want to taste it for myself; do to me what you have done to Bonelwa!" she demanded in her drunken voice.

Tau looked at her in disbelief, and wondered if this was the same Zuki that he knew, but he knew it was the alcohol talking. He turned away from her and headed toward the door.

"Let me take you to your room and forget this ever happened," he said, looking at the door.

However, there was no answer nor stumbling steps following after him, so he turned back and saw Zuki naked. His eyes popped out as he looked at Zuki's nakedness; after looking at her with lust for a while, he turned his eyes away in shame.

"Zuki, please put on your clothes!" he demanded.

Zuki moved toward him, and held him from behind and whispered in his ears, "Don't tell me you don't want me, I've noticed how you look at me with lust, even when I am with Bonelwa. Now, please don't tell me it never crossed your mind?"

Tau was too weak at this point to give her an answer.

"This will be our little secret, if you don't tell Bonelwa, I won't," she enticed him.

"It is not right," Tau's conscience said, but his body protested.

Zuki stretched out her hand and inappropriately touched Tau.

"I don't want to hurt Bonelwa," he mumbled in weakness, with his mouth in one place and his body in another.

"What she doesn't know can never hurt her," persisted the determined seductress.

By the time Tau turned back to face her, Zuki intensified her seduction. Zuki suggested doing things to him that conservative Bonelwa would never consider, let alone agree!

Zuki gave Tau full access to her body and encouraged him to indulge without restraint. The two spent whatever was left of the night together fulfilling their wildest fantasies, unrestrained.

They spent four days in Tau's room, without going out; they could not keep their hands off each other.

Bonelwa kept looking at her phone for a text message or a call from Tau, but there was no sign of him. They never spent hours without texting each other, let alone a day. Four days was just more than she could bear! So she called him and to her annoyance, Tau's phone went straight to voicemail.

Tau's battery died, Zuki kept him so busy that he forgot to charge his phone.

Bonelwa's happy holiday was quickly turning into a regrettable trip.

On the fifth day, Tau returned her call and lied to her, telling her that he was busy studying, and that he forgot to charge his phone and apologized. Bonelwa reluctantly forgave him and gave him the benefit of the doubt, though her womanly instinct knew something was terribly wrong; she just could not point it out from Eastern Cape.

Unable to contain her anxiety any longer, she decided to return to Cape Town without telling Tau. When she arrived at the campus, she went straight to Tau's room, and knocked on the door. Tau opened the door expecting to see Zuki playing one of her sexual games, but to his surprise, it was Bonelwa.

"Hey, Baby, I thought you were still…." He swallowed hard and his brain stopped functioning for a while.

"Are you going to invite me in or are you going to leave me standing here at the door?" Bonelwa reacted, irritated at his cold reception.

"Yes, sure, come on in," he replied, hoping that Zuki didn't leave any clothes or sexual gadgets laying around.

Bonelwa entered the room with her eyes thoroughly scanning the room for any foreign elements, but she couldn't find anything unusual, apart from Tau's stinking guilty behavior.

"What's wrong, Baby?" Tau asked, trying to diffuse the tension in the highly charged room.

"I don't know, you tell me," she retorted, waiting to catch him lying.

Tau's eyes almost came out of his head, and his heart grew cold with fear, when he spotted Zuki's red g-string lying next to his bed, partially covered by his bed sheet. He tried to divert Bonelwa's attention from there.

"Let's go somewhere else and grab a drink or something and talk about whatever is bothering you," he suggested, trying to get Bonelwa out of the room as soon as possible.

"What's wrong with talking here?" Bonelwa protested, unimpressed. "We always talk here for hours, what the hell is going on, Tau?!"

"What do you mean?" he mumbled through his guilty lips.

"Let me see... you didn't call or text me for four consecutive days and I come here, after spending several days apart from you, and you open the door, give me no hug or kiss and leave me hanging at the door like some stranger—not to mention that you keep on acting all guilty like someone who is hiding something. Who is in here with you, Tau?" she shouted, and started searching the small room. When she tried to look under the bed, Tau stopped her.

"Stop it, Baby. There is nothing wrong and there is no one in here," he tried to make her feel as if she was some crazy, jealous, out-of-control girlfriend.

"But... why are you acting so weird and all guilty? You have changed, Tau. When I left, you were so in love with me, I could feel your love from a distance, and you almost convinced me not to go and visit my family, so that we could spend the holiday together. You didn't want us to be apart from each other, and then, all of a sudden you ignore me for four days as if I don't exist! What has changed since I left, Tau, please tell me?" she burst into tears.

Tau quickly grabbed Zuki's g-string and put it into his pocket while she was distracted crying, then went and sat next to her.

"There is nothing wrong, and I still love you... I guess I was just too preoccupied with studying for my upcoming final exams. I am sorry, Baby, please forgive me," he lied, feeling guilty for putting her under such distressing circumstances.

Bonelwa knew he was lying, yet at that very moment, she was unwilling to face the bitter truth. So, she opted to convince herself to believe the sweet lie, because at that very moment, it tasted much better than the bitter truth.

While they proceeded to talk things through, Tau continued to deny and lie as Bonelwa put forth her concerns and suspicions.

Zuki, who went out to get pizza for herself and Tau, returned to Tau's room. When she got to the door, she heard Bonelwa's voice talking to Tau; upon hearing her voice, Zuki ran with all her might to her room and locked the door behind her, as if somehow, that would ease her guilty mind for betraying her best friend so fatally.

Bonelwa left Tau's room to give him time to study and prepare for his exams and went to her room.

When she arrived at her room, she was heavy-hearted and she needed someone to talk to and unwind her mind, but because Zuki told her that she was also going to visit her family, she felt all alone.

She cried herself to sleep out of regret, finally falling asleep with a sorrowful heart, though nothing was yet confirmed. Deep down, Bonelwa knew that whatever she would eventually find out, would not be good news for her, and it would alter her relationship with Tau; the mere thought of parting ways with Tau was tearing up her severely wounded heart.

CHAPTER TWO

She got up early in the morning hoping that it was just her insecurities that were causing all the distress that was troubling her gentle soul. So she decided to forget about it and pretend that it didn't happen. Bonelwa headed to the cafeteria to grab coffee and something to eat, on her way there, some guys and girls looked at her with pity, while others whispered as she passed by. By the time she arrived at the cafeteria, she knew that her nightmare was a glaring reality—Tau had indeed cheated on her! "But with who?" she wondered out loud.

She left the cafeteria with her coffee and breakfast, deciding to go and lock herself in her room and stay there for a couple of days. She felt deeply humiliated, and her self-esteem was almost non-existent; and even though she was very beautiful, she felt ugly and unattractive.

On her way to her room, she spotted Zuki from afar on the other side of the campus. She was glad that her best friend was back, so she ran toward Zuki and met up with her as she was about to enter her room.

"Zuki! Wait up…" she shouted trying to catch her breath.

Zuki was unsure if by now Bonelwa knew of her betrayal.

"Hey, I didn't know you were back already! What are you doing here? Aren't you supposed to be in Eastern Cape or something?" Zuki lied, trying to deflect attention from her guilty self.

"It's a long story, I will tell you all about it in a minute, just let me drink some water first," Bonelwa replied, entering Zuki's room. She took a bottle of water and sat on Zuki's bed to catch her breath.

With her thirst quenched, she looked at her best friend with tearful eyes.

Zuki realized she was not yet aware of her betrayal.

"So what's going on?" she asked pretending to be concerned.

"I don't know where to start… Tau took me to the airport, deeply in love with me. I stayed four days in Eastern Cape and didn't get a single text or call from him while there, which is so unlike him. I come back here and he is completely out of love with me—and worst of all, I am sure he is having an affair! What did I do wrong, Zuki?" Bonelwa asked, crying.

"Are you sure he is having an affair? Maybe he is just stressed-out about his exams," Zuki offered her traitorous comfort.

"No, Zuki! He's having an affair; I am positive about it. Everybody who knows us seems to know; they're all whispering and talking behind my back. Tau is cheating on me, Zuki…" Bonelwa affirmed.

"Am I ugly and unattractive? What does she have, whoever she is, that I don't have—that she stole his heart away from me so rapidly?" Bonelwa sobbed.

"I am so sorry Bonelwa, that bastard is not worthy of you. You must dump that cheating bastard!" Zuki mocked Bonelwa.

"Part of me wants to do just that, but the other part just wants him to love me again and for things to return to the way they were before I left," Bonelwa poured out her heart.

"Girl, if he cheated on you as you affirm he did, things will never be the same again!" Zuki insisted.

"I guess you are right, and I don't think I can forgive him at this stage, but the most painful thing to me is that, I don't think he even wants to be forgiven," Bonelwa conceded and started crying her broken heart out.

Zuki went and sat next to Bonelwa.

"Come here, Girl, it's going to be fine," Zuki offered Bonelwa her shoulder to lean on and a tissue to wipe her tears away.

They spent that day inside Zuki's room, though all along Zuki wanted Bonelwa to leave. However, she craftily played the best friend part until Bonelwa left her room.

Bonelwa lay on her bed thinking about whether she should confront Tau about it or if she should just soldier on, let it go, and try to win her man back.

After a long conversation with herself, she decided that she would try to win him back; so she got up from her moping bed, took a shower, dressed up, put on her makeup and headed for Tau's room. When she got there, he was not there. After waiting for a long while, she gave up hoping that he would return that night. So sulking, she headed to the only place where she thought she could find some comfort, and knocked at the door.

"Who is it?" a voice called from inside the room.

"Open the door, who do you think it is?" Bonelwa shouted.

"Okay, I'm coming… just a second," the voice replied from within.

The door opened and Bonelwa burst into the room, saying, "Girl, I need something strong to drink my pain away!"

"What's wrong and why are you all dressed up?" Zuki asked.

"I decided to forgive him and let it go. I went there to remind him of what we had not so long ago, and see if maybe we could patch things up!" Bonelwa replied.

"And?" Zuki asked.

"And the bastard is not even there! I am sure they are together right now and maybe they are even... oh, I can't take this anymore, I need something strong! What do you have in here?" Bonelwa complained.

"Stop it, Bonelwa! You can't destroy your life just because a man cheated on you, and besides you don't even drink; get yourself together and move on!" Zuki said brazenly.

"I can't just move on, Zuki, he is my first love, the one I intended to love for the rest of my life! My life is over, all my dreams and plans are shattered, and I just don't know what to do..." Bonelwa cried, approaching Zuki, seeking her friend's shoulder to lean on. Zuki felt pity for her. She felt a deep sense of guilt seeing Bonelwa torn into pieces like that, so she opened her arms and said, "I am so sorry, Bonelwa, come here Girl."

Bonelwa ran to her like a crying child runs to a mother to find comfort in her mother's arms. They hugged each other and Bonelwa cried freely on Zuki's shoulder, and rested there with her eyes closed.

She was awakened, as someone who was having a nightmare, when she smelled Tau's cologne on Zuki. She pushed Zuki as far away from her as possible.

"What the hell? No! It can't be you! How could you, Zuki? How could you do this to me?" Bonelwa cried bitter tears.

"What are talking about, Girl?" Zuki tried to conceal her distress.

"Where is he?" Bonelwa asked, rushing to check under Zuki's bed… and there was Tau hiding!

"Really Tau? Why? How could you do this to us? I gave you all of myself and this is how you love me back?" she shouted.

Before Tau could answer, anger got the best of her and without thinking she took off her high heel and started hitting Tau with it as hard as she could.

"Bonelwa, please stop it, you going to hurt me," Tau pled.

"I don't just want to hurt you, Tau, I want to kill you with my heels! I want you to feel the pain of my broken heart!" she shouted back at him, while she hit him with more rage.

"Bonelwa, you don't mean it, please stop it, I am bleeding!" Tau begged.

Bonelwa looked at her heel, it was full of blood. She stopped hitting him and turned her ferocious gaze on Zuki, who at this stage was shrivelling with fear. She had never seen gentle Bonelwa this angry in all the time that they've known each other.

Holding her high heel with her right hand, drops of blood falling from it, she approached Zuki, pointing at her with her left index finger, she said, "You, Little Slut, are deserving of death right now!"

Bonelwa was shorter in stature, compared to Zuki, yet Zuki shrieked in fear and sat next to the wall and covered her face with her hands.

"Please don't hit me, please… I'm very sorry," Zuki begged.

Bonelwa looked at her and said, "I feel sorry for you, if this is what you do to someone who you claim is your best friend. I wonder what you do to your enemies! Here I was pouring my heart to you, while all along you were mocking me in your heart. You are nothing but a masquerading prostitute that takes advantage of men's weaknesses."

"Bonelwa, please calm down and let's talk about it," Tau pleaded from behind her.

"There is nothing to talk about!" she shouted at Tau, her eyes fixed on Zuki.

Bonelwa pulled Zuki by the hair and dragged her from where she was sitting into the centre of the room, and laid her at Tau's feet.

"Here is your little slut, you deserve each other!" she shouted at Tau.

"Baby, please sit down and let us talk about this," Tau begged.

"Don't call me 'Baby'—I'm not your 'Baby', you bastard!" she shouted.

"Baby, please…" Tau implored.

"Cheater, please don't 'Baby' me!" she said, agitated.

"Baby…"

Before he could say please, Bonelwa forcefully threw the high heel at him, but Tau ducked and the shoe missed him.

"Tau, if I hear one more 'Baby, please' coming from your dirty and cheating lips, I will not be responsible for what happens after that!" she warned him.

"Okay…" Tau conceded for fear of the enraged petite woman.

"It's all my fault, I'm the one that seduced him," Zuki confessed from the floor.

"So what? Is that supposed to make me feel better?" she shouted. "I don't care which one of you seduced the other, all I know is that the two of you broke my trust. Come to think of it, you deserve each other, and as far as I am concerned, you're both dead to me! May the two of you rot in hell!" she yelled at them and stormed out of the room,

Bonelwa left her gentle and conservative self behind her, the Bonelwa that went into that room died there and was buried in that room.

Broken and exceedingly enraged she left and went to her room, feeling empty inside. Her mind ran to and fro trying to find a way to avenge herself and make the two of them feel as much pain as she could inflict on them. When she arrived at her room, instead of crying, she hardened her heart, took a pair of scissors and grabbed the photobook. She went through it looking for photos of Zuki, Tau and herself, and she found many; she sat on her bed and started to cut out Zuki and Tau from all the photos. It took her almost two hours to finish all the photos, yet her hand wasn't tired of cutting their faces from the photos, she was only sad that there were no more photos with their faces to cut out. The cutting made her feel good. She felt as if, somehow, she had physically removed them from her life and erased them from her memory.

The following day she called her mother and told her mother everything. Worried, her mother sent her a plane ticket for the next available flight to Eastern Cape, which was in the early hours of the morning on the day after. Her mother, Fezeka, picked her from the airport and took her to a park where they could talk freely without being overheard by her overly conservative father and two extremely protective brothers.

"Oh, Nelwa… I am so sorry for all that these two people who call themselves your friends have done to you. Are you okay?" Fezeka asked.

"I am fine, Mom," she replied, keeping the attitude and position she took… never to be a victim again, but to be strong and hard-hearted.

"Are you disappointed in me, for losing my virginity before marriage?" she asked her worried mother.

"Yes, I am very disappointed!" Fezeka replied. "After all our discussions, I expected better from you, Bonelwa! Virginity is the best gift you can give to your husband! My grandmother married as a virgin, my mother married as a virgin, I married as a virgin and I hoped you would continue the tradition and pass it to your daughters! But now, you've broken a long-held family tradition. How am I going to look at your mother-in-law's face when she discovers that you were not a virgin when you married her son? And what are you going to tell your husband? 'Sorry Honey, I'm damaged goods?' I am very disappointed in you, but you are my daughter and I love you no matter what."

"I am very sorry for disappointing you, Mom, please forgive me," Bonelwa apologized.

"I forgive you my daughter," Fezeka replied.

"Thank you, Mamma, your forgiveness means a lot to me. I just wish I could turn back the time and keep my virginity and give it to my husband, whoever he will be," Bonelwa said with regret.

"Unfortunately, that is not possible. There are things in life, which you only get to do once and there are no second chances, whatever you do with them stays that way, until you die! Virginity is one of them—you mess up once and it is forever messed up," Fezeka admonished her daughter. Then, she hugged Bonelwa, comforted her, and then looking at her, she said, "Let us go home," and they left the park.

CHAPTER THREE

The holiday was over and Bonelwa returned to campus. She tried her best to focus on her studies, but she could not resist the overwhelming urge to keep tabs on Tau and Zuki, so she started spying on them. The more she watched them happy together, the angrier and more resentful she became of them.

Her love for Tau quickly turned into hatred. The hate she felt for Tau was so strong, it surpassed the love that she'd had for him. She had one desire, and one desire only—to see a jealous look on Tau's face when he sees her happy with another guy. She didn't care who, as long as together they could attract Tau's attention, make him jealous, and regret ever choosing Zuki over her.

So, she started hanging with the wrong crowds—the party people on campus. Soon, she was invited by a new friend to attend a bedroom party at Eric's room, an international student of British nationality. At the party, she saw her fellow students sniffing cocaine, smoking weed and wasting themselves away with alcohol. As the party progressed, she was horrified to witness the couples in the room doing things to each other right in front of everybody, yet nobody seemed to be bothered, apart from her.

"What am I doing here?" she questioned herself and the wisdom of her retaliation plan. Yet, blinded by pain and hatred, she soldiered on. Even though she was shocked at the environment in which she found herself, she reasoned with herself that is was better than her own conservative environment where she had to constantly explain what had happened between her and Tau. She was sick to the stomach and tired of being the subject of pity. She didn't want pity, she wanted revenge. She wanted Tau and Zuki to regret messing with the wrong girl! She desperately wanted her payback time.

Although the environment and the company she was keeping was vile and corrupt, she cared not, so long as it advanced her rancorous plan.

Her mind returned to the room. She saw that, out of the ten people in the room, there was three couples, and two other people spent most of their time with each other and they seemed to be into each other, so that left her and the host as the only people unpaired in the room.

Eric was tall, well built, dark and very handsome; he was a catalogue model and an aspiring actor. Bonelwa checked him out throughout the night, not because she was into him, but because she saw in him her perfect weapon to make Tau jealous.

By the time she left the party, she had her plan all figured out.

Two days later, on a Friday, she saw Tau and Zuki heading out of campus, and she followed them at a distance, watched them enter a nearby coffee shop and saw where they were seated. She rushed back to campus, quickly changed and went straight to Eric's room. When she got to the door, she felt she shouldn't do it, but after having a conversation with herself, she decided to go ahead with the plan. Just before she knocked on the door, she took a mirror from her handbag, checked herself in the mirror to make sure that she was looking her very best and after some final touches, she confidently knocked on the door. She waited a bit, but there was no answer, so she decided to knock again, while looking left and right making sure no one was seeing her. When she tried to knock again, Eric opened the door to let a girl out.

"Thanks, I hope to see you again soon!" the girl said on her way out.

She met Bonelwa at the door, "Hi, I didn't know there was a line today! You will not regret it, he is totally worth the effort and the waiting!" the girl announced to Bonelwa.

"Sure, thanks for the info!" Bonelwa retorted and rolled her eyes.

"Hi, Bonelwa, right?" Eric asked, trying to make sure.

"Yep, the one and only," she replied, trying to conceal her desperation.

"Come on in," Eric invited.

"I would prefer we talk somewhere else, if you don't mind," she suggested, trying not to offend him.

"No problem, I understand, let me just grab a shirt," he said, entering his room and coming out in a dash.

"So where do you want to talk?" he asked.

"How about you let me buy you a cup of coffee and we talk over coffee, like in the good old days," she replied.

"Okay, I see, I can do that," he was up to the challenge.

Eric was the non-committal type of guy, his good looks made him proud and selfish; he thought he was too good looking to be committed to just one girl, so he opted for freelance dating, offering his time and affection to any girl that needed it. He was loyal to no one but himself and his desires, and what made him more confident in his selfish ways, was that the girls were fine with sharing him openly.

Bonelwa couldn't care less who he dated, or how many people he dated, so long as she got a chance to use him to make Tau regret his decision to leave her. So she took Eric to the coffee shop where Tau and Zuki were, and she asked the waiter to seat them next to Tau's and Zuki's table. The waiter led them to their table. Bonelwa held Eric's hand and Eric unknowingly played along as he always did with other girls. Once they were seated and placed their orders, Bonelwa tried her best to pretend as if she didn't see Tau and Zuki. Zuki didn't see Bonelwa, she was sitting facing the opposite direction, but Tau saw her. However, Bonelwa strategically sat with her back facing Tau, giving him a full view of her weapon—Eric.

Seeing Bonelwa looking very pretty and holding hands with Eric, Tau felt a bit jealous. However, he felt more guilty than jealous because he knew Eric and the type of people he hangs with, so he thought that maybe Bonelwa was also doing drugs and drinking. He felt responsible for driving Bonelwa into the arms of the likes of Eric, and that distracted him from the conversation he was having with Zuki.

"Baby, what do you think about that? Do you like it?" Zuki asked.

"I am sorry Baby, what do I think about what?" Tau asked, confused.

"About what I have been speaking about for the past five minutes, what's wrong with you, Tau? Where is your mind?" Zuki demanded.

"I am sorry Baby, my mind was preoccupied with something else. Could you please repeat it from the beginning?" Tau asked, but his eyes were still fixed on Bonelwa and Eric.

"What is so special behind me that you keep on looking at it and has distracted you from our life plans?" Zuki asked, turning back to see what had distracted Tau.

"I see... very important indeed," Zuki said.

"Baby, can we please leave now and finish our conversation in your room?" Tau suggested.

"No, Tau! I am not going to run away and put our life on hold, every time we see Bonelwa with some guy!" Zuki shouted.

"Shush... Baby, please keep it down," Tau begged.

"Don't shush me, Tau! If you want me to be quiet, give me the attention that I deserve!" she shouted louder, to the disturbance of the other customers.

"Okay, Baby, I am sorry. You have my full attention now," he conceded.

While he was still talking, Eric got up from his chair and kissed Bonelwa's neck; Tau got uncomfortable with that.

"Tau!" Zuki shouted, "What must I do for you to keep your eyes on me? Must I get naked here, will that help? I can do that, if that would help you fix your eyes on me as you have them fixed on other people's business!" she demanded.

"I am sorry Baby, please can we go now?" Tau replied.

"Yes, we can go now, but you are going straight to your room and I am going to mine," Zuki announced and stormed out of the restaurant.

Bonelwa, who was watching all the action in a reflection on the glass wall facing her, couldn't be happier.

Tau settled the bill and went out, head down. After he left, ten minutes later, Bonelwa also asked for the bill.

"Why do you want to go now? I am enjoying myself," Eric asked, perplexed.

"Me too, but I forgot I have a test tomorrow. Can we please go now?" Bonelwa replied, settling the bill.

"Okay Baby, whatever you want," Eric was not pleased.

"Can ask you a favor?" she asked.

"Yes, anything Baby," he replied.

"Please don't call me 'Baby', call me anything else, but 'Baby', I hate the word 'Baby'!" she requested.

"Okay, Baby...sorry, it slipped out. Yes, no problem, I will find something else to call you, maybe Pumpkin?" Eric said jokingly in his British accent.

"Pumpkin is perfect!" Bonelwa agreed. And they left the restaurant and went back to the campus.

Eric went to his room, challenged; he usually got the girl in his bed on the first day. So he was excited at the idea that Bonelwa was playing hard to get.

Bonelwa went to her room, celebrating, her "first mission accomplished!" and she patted herself on the back.

When she arrived at her room, she found Tau waiting for her.

"What are you doing here, Tau?" she asked with a cold and calm voice.

"I just wanted to make sure that you are fine," Tau replied.

"Really?" she exclaimed.

"Yes, really! Bonelwa, I know I've hurt you, and I'm very sorry for hurting you, please forgive me. But please don't destroy your life! Eric is no good for you!" he warned.

"Let me be the judge of that," she replied.

"Bonelwa, you don't know him, he is going to use and hurt you badly!" he pleaded with her to listen.

"Like you did? At least he will not have my virginity on his conscience! Like some fool that hurt me!" she answered back.

"I didn't plan to cheat on you, let alone fall for Zuki, it just happened, please believe me, I did not do it to hurt you on purpose, you must believe me, Bonelwa!" Tau pleaded.

"Okay, I believe you, can you go back to your slut now? Oh, I forgot, she stormed out on you!" she responded with a sarcastic laugh.

"Bonelwa, doing drugs, smoking weed, and drinking alcohol will not solve anything, it will only destroy your life!" Tau cautioned, concerned.

"What life, Tau? The one you have destroyed? That one was destroyed by you, Tau! There is no life left for me, you have killed it! Can you please leave!" she shouted at him.

Fearing the argument might attract unwanted attention from other fellow students, Tau left to his room feeling guilty.

CHAPTER FOUR

Bonelwa continued to stalk Tau and Zuki, spending as much time as she could with Eric, desperately trying to rub her fake happiness in Tau's face at every opportunity.

One day, she saw Tau and Zuki laying on the grass in the park nearby, on the very spot where she and Tau used to gaze at the stars together while holding hands. Seeing them there opened the wounds of betrayal in her heart afresh. She felt like going there and confronting Tau for taking Zuki to the place she introduced him to, but pride would not let her do it; she didn't want to be seen as a crazy, bitter ex-girlfriend. So she ran to the campus and went straight to Eric's room with intention of taking him there, since that was her spot in the first place.

When she arrived at the door, she tried to catch her breath before knocking. After composing herself, she looked at herself in her secret mirror and did some touch ups to her hair and put on some perfume, just in case the running added an unwanted odour to her person. She knocked and Eric opened the door.

"Hi," she greeted him, trying not to seem as though she came to fetch him as her weapon of war.

"Hey, look who is here! Ms. Hard-To-Get!" Eric was high on weed.

She smiled to conceal her impatient agenda, and said, "Wanna go for a walk in the park? It is a beautiful night!"

"Baby, why don't we skip your little games tonight and let me give you what you really came here for," he replied and pulled her inside, locking the door behind them.

"What's got into you? Are you high, or what?" she complained.

"Stop talking, Baby, and take off your clothes!" he demanded.

"This is not funny, Eric! Please open the door and let me out!" she shouted.

"C'mon on, Baby, I know you want me, stop playing hard to get," he insisted.

"No, Eric, I don't want you, please let me go!" She demanded.

"Oh, I see… you're the type that likes it rough," he said taking his clothes off. She tried to run to the door, but he blocked her way and pushed her down on his bed.

"Eric, please stop and let me go," she begged him.

"Not until you got what you came here for," he replied.

"I did not come here for sex!" she shouted.

"Of course you did, otherwise, why would you be coming here all the time? I know your type; you are a good girl that wants to taste what is like to be with a bad boy. Well, let me give you a taste," he said, taking off his underwear.

"No, I don't! Help! Somebody please help!" she shouted at the top of her voice, but Eric turned up the volume of his stereo to block her cry for help.

He then forcefully violated her. Though initially she fought with all her might and tried to pull him off her, she was unable. Overpowered and in shock, her system shut down and she became numb. Eric continued to help himself until he had satisfied his lust. He looked at Bonelwa, expecting her to say something. There was no sound coming from her, the only words she spoke were the sad tears rolling down her inanimate eyes, and that is when he realized what he had done.

After laying there in a state of shock for a good while, she took courage and left his room. Once again, whatever fragment of human affection she had left, was left behind her in that room.

When she arrived at her room, she wanted to call the police, but the thought of having Tau, Zuki and the whole campus hear about it was enough to stop her from calling the cops. The dread of shame and humiliation made her keep the rape to herself. She was not prepared to endure public humiliation, so she decided to toughen up and harden her heart against men. She blamed herself and felt guilty. She tried to convince herself that it was partly her fault, and that she should never have gone into his room in the first place. So deeply angry with herself, she felt dirty. She entered the shower with her clothes on and took a long shower trying to wash away the dirt. She spent the next three days indoors. On the fourth day after the rape, she decided to attend classes. She became bitter and suspicious every time she saw people whispering.

When she returned that day from attending classes, she made a vow to herself, that she would never again have female friends and that she would make all men pay for what Tau and Eric did to her.

A few weeks later, still nursing her broken heart and violated body, she sat on the grass in the campus reading a book. Her reading was interrupted by a freshman named Senzo.

"Hi, do you mind if I sit next to you?" Senzo asked.

She looked at him standing right in front of her, blocking the sun.

"No, I don't mind," she retorted.

"Thanks... I'm Senzo... it's my first year," he introduced himself.

"I'm Bonelwa," she stretched her hand to shake his hand.

"Nice meeting you, Bonelwa!" He shook her hand.

"Nice to meet you too, Senzo!" she retorted.

"Let me not take any more of your time, happy reading!" he said grabbing a book from his bag and sat next to her.

"Thank you," she replied.

After two uninterrupted hours, Senzo, noticing that Bonelwa had stopped reading, asked, "What's the book about?"

"It's a book about how to spot a cheater, a player, the noncommittal, the violent, the abuser and all the other types of men," she responded.

"Hmmm... I didn't know there was such a book! Who wrote it? Is it even possible to do that?" he asked, perplexed.

"It's written by a psychologist, who studied men's behavior for over twenty years," she replied.

"Okay... interesting," Senzo retorted.

As they continued to talk, Bonelwa started warming up to Senzo, even though he was two years younger than her. Senzo was very smart, handsome and funny, qualities she loved in men.

After six days of interacting with each other, Senzo asked Bonelwa to go out with him on a movie date, and she accepted. Most girls cried throughout the emotionally charged movie, but there was not a single tear from Bonelwa's eyes. Many girls leaned on their partner's shoulders, but she sat there unmoved. When they arrived back at the campus, Senzo walked her to her room, said goodnight, and they departed from each. Two days later, on Friday night, Senzo came to Bonelwa's room, dressed to impress, he knocked on Bonelwa's door.

"Hi," she greeted.

"Hi, I wanted to surprise you tonight, if you are free I would like to take you out for dinner," he proposed.

Bonelwa pulled him inside the room and locked the door behind them and pushed him into the wall.

"Why don't we skip dinner? "She said in a seductive voice.

"Okay..." Senzo replied, shocked and thrilled at the same time.

She then grabbed him and threw him on her bed and said, "Let's skip drinks and dessert as well, and let me give you what you really came here for."

"No! Bonelwa, I didn't come here for sex," he protested.

Before he could finish talking, Bonelwa took her dress off, she was not wearing any undies. Senzo's eyes almost popped out! And he couldn't talk for a while.

"Why are you still dressed up, don't you want it?" she asked.

"Bonelwa, there is something I need to tell..." he mumbled.

"What is it, Senzo?" she asked with her eyes wide open.

"I... I... I never..." the words would not come out.

"You've never been with a girl before?" she tried to help him talk.

"Yes, I have never been with a girl before," he confirmed, looking down.

"It's okay, don't be afraid, I'm not going to bite you," she assured him, rubbing her hands on his chest.

"Take your pants off," she requested.

Senzo got under the sheets and complied. He threw his pants on the other side of the bed.

"You are a shy boy, aren't you?"

Senzo nodded his head in agreement.

"Okay, do you want me to switch off the light for you?" she tried to get him to relax.

Senzo nodded, "yes" with his head.

She switched off the light and joined him under the sheets and right there, Senzo got his virginity snipped away from him.

The following day, after classes, Senzo went to the nearby florist and got some red roses for Bonelwa, and rushed to her room, his heart filled with love and youthful infatuation. He was eager to prove to Bonelwa that he was not just after sex.

When he got to the door, he took his breath freshener, sprayed it into his mouth and knocked on the door. Bonelwa opened the door wearing nothing but a bath towel wrapped around her body; she had just taken a shower and was about to get dressed when Senzo knocked on her door. Senzo could smell the fresh scent of her perfumed shampoo, mesmerized, he said, "Hi, these are for you."

"Wow! Cute, very cute, thank you!" she said taking the flowers from his hands.

Senzo kissed her on the neck, while handing over the flowers, and he entered the room.

"Wow! I'm very impressed, Senzo! You are very smooth, like a real Casanova, and for that, you get a reward!" She locked the door behind her and dropped the towel saying, "Come, touch me everywhere, I am all yours."

"I…" Senzo wanted to voice that he wanted to take her out, but Bonelwa's gorgeous body interfered with his thinking.

"Never mind that," he said, moving toward her, and with his hands, he said yes to her invitation. That night he did not return to his room; Bonelwa spent the night initiating him into the world of adults.

After weeks of intense dating, Senzo was convinced that Bonelwa was his soulmate. After meditating the whole day, searching for the most meaningful and appropriate words to describe his love to Bonelwa, he found none. So, he decided to declare his love to Bonelwa from the heart, no script.

When his last class ended, he rushed to his room, called the five-star restaurant to confirm the reservation he had made two days ago, and to his delight, his table for two was still reserved under his name. As the sun set, he freshened up and put on his favourite jeans and jacket, got a red rose on his way to Bonelwa's room and confidently knocked on the door. Bonelwa opened the door half way.

"Tonight is the night…" Senzo sang joyfully to her.

"What's going on? And why are you all dressed up?" Bonelwa asked.

"It's a surprise, Baby, all I need you to do is put on your best evening dress and that perfume of yours that I love so much, and we'll be heading to our destination," Senzo replied, his eyes filled with happiness.

"Senzo, we need to talk," Bonelwa retorted.

"Yes, I agree. We'll talk at our destination… but right now let me help you get ready, we must not be late," Senzo replied, trying to get into the room. But Bonelwa stopped him by putting her hand on the door post.

"You can't come in, Senzo, we need to talk right here," she said in a serious tone of voice.

"Why? What's going on, Bonelwa?" he asked, agitated.

"Nothing is going on, Senzo, and there is no one in here, in case you are wondering," she said, opening the door wide so that he could gaze inside.

"So why can't I come in then?" he asked, a bit relieved.

"Senzo, it was fun while it lasted, but we must stop seeing each other," she dropped the bomb as gently and calmly as she could.

A cold silence swept the corridor, as Senzo tried to process what he had just heard.

"It was fun! I can't believe this, what about the connection we had? Was that also just a funny game you were playing?" he responded in disbelief.

"Senzo, you had a connection with me, but I didn't have a connection with you, and that has nothing to do with you, it has to do with me," she said, trying to get him to accept it.

"How could you not have a connection with me after all those lovely times we spent together? We were almost inseparable, what really happened, Bonelwa?"

"Senzo, to have a connection with someone, one needs a heart, and it's clear I don't have a heart right now. My heart was broken and shattered into pieces, and even if wanted to, it is impossible for me to have the connection that you want and deserve," she said, almost in tears.

"Bonelwa, you let me be the judge of who is worthy of my love," he responded. Looking at her in the eye, he said, "We can work something out, I can give you some time for your heart to heal and then we will be happy together, Bonelwa."

"Senzo, I don't want you to put your life on hold for me. You are a great guy—the best—and some other time, or in another planet, maybe you and I could be perfect for each other, but right now on this planet called reality, if we continue together, you will only get deeply hurt, and I cannot have that on my conscience."

"That is a risk I am willing to take, if you just let me."

"No, Senzo, I can't let you throw away your chance to be happy, for something we are not even sure will ever happen. Please go and find someone who is perfect for you."

"I have already found my perfect one."

"No, Senzo, a real one that feels the same way about you; besides, you are still very young, you will quickly forget about me."

"Never, Bonelwa! I may move on with my life, but forget you… that will never happen."

"Oh Senzo… please don't make it more difficult than it already is."

"I won't, I will be leaving shortly, but before I go, please look at me."

She looked at him, their eyes locked, as if they both could see into each other's soul; he then brushed her hair backwards with his left hand and caressed her right cheek with his right hand and said, "This is not youthful infatuation, this is true love; I will love again, true, but no one will ever make me feel the way you do, you are my soulmate, Bonelwa. You must take care of yourself… bye my perfect one." He kissed her on the forehead and left, nursing the first heart-break of his life.

Bonelwa, stood there at the door watching him go, wondering if she would regret letting Senzo go for the rest of her life; but her pain and desire to make Tau and Zuki pay was stronger than the fear of a life of regret. So she closed the door and hardened her heart and decided to forge ahead with her plan of revenge.

CHAPTER FIVE

our days later, still nursing his broken heart and trying to make sense of the puzzle, Senzo decided to take a walk and read a book in the campus' garden. When he arrived there, he found Bonelwa sitting in the place where they first met. His heart deeply longed for her and he desperately wanted to reach out to her and say hello, but his male ego would not let him, so he found a hidden spot and sat there.

Bonelwa's reading was interrupted by loud laughs that sounded familiar to her. Curious, her eyes followed the voices and they were led almost outside the garden, where Eric was having an excited conversation with his best friend, Langa Ndongeni, who happened to be the captain of the soccer team on campus. Langa was also the face and ambassador of one of the most popular and influential non-profit organizations that advocated against abuse and violence against women and children. Eric and Langa were best friends since they were little; Langa's parents were expats in England for almost twenty years. When Langa decided to attend the University of Cape Town, Eric decided to join him. They graduated from high school together and did almost everything together; their dream was to graduate from university on the same day, if possible. They were that close.

Bonelwa watched Eric and wished that she could wipe away that happy smile on the rapist's face. Angry, she returned to her room and contemplated the possibility of telling the police what Eric had done to her, but the thought of her parents being embarrassed in their conservative circles, restrained her desire for justice.

"He'll pay, one way or the other, I will make sure of that... I'll give him a taste of my pain!" she said to herself as she moved up and down in her room.

A week later, Eric went to Langa's room to walk him to his soccer practice, as he always did. He tried to get into his room, but to his surprise it was locked. Langa never locked his door during the day, because he didn't like to be disturbed when he was sitting or lying on the bed. Eric came to his room many times a day.

Eric knocked on the door, and the door was opened. He looked in disbelief when he saw Bonelwa on the other side of the door, wearing nothing but Langa's soccer jersey.

"What are you doing here?" he demanded. She gave him no answer.

He pushed her out of the way, and got into the room shouting, "Langa, what is this thing doing here?"

"What thing?" Langa answered, still half asleep.

"This thing!" he pointed at Bonelwa.

"Eric, please don't be rude; this is my girlfriend, Bonelwa," Langa replied.

Looking at Bonelwa, Langa said, "Bonelwa, this is my best friend Eric, please don't mind him, he can be a piece of work at times."

"Yes, I know him," Bonelwa replied.

"Your girlfriend? Please tell me you are joking, you are the captain of the soccer team, you cannot go out with this trash!" Eric disapproved.

"Eric, please calm down. What's gotten into you today? Why are you so worked up?" Langa asked.

"Langa, please listen to me, you cannot date this tramp, she is not worth it, trust me Bro," Eric insisted.

"Eric, please stop calling her names, you don't even know her!" Langa raised his voice.

"Oh yes… I know her, she is a whore!" Eric responded.

"I don't know what has gotten into you today, but I think it is better if you leave my room now!" Langa, upset, opened the door to let Eric out.

"What? There is no way I am leaving—this tramp must go and leave us alone!" he shouted, forcefully grabbing Bonelwa's left arm with intention to push her out of the room.

"Let me go!" Bonelwa shouted, freeing herself with all her might.

She was left with bruises on her arm. When Langa saw the bruises, he aggressively pushed Eric away from her, and said, "What are you doing, man? Have you gone mad or what?"

"I am not mad, but this tramp is coming between us," he replied.

"Eric!" Langa angrily shouted, walking away from him and turning around to check out on Bonelwa.

"Are you okay? I am so sorry about all this, let me get some ice for your bruises."

"It's okay, Langa… there are many things you don't know about your so-called best friend, and he knows that if you find out who he really is, you would stop hanging out with him. So, the fear of me telling you who he really is, is driving him mad," Bonelwa replied.

"What do you mean? What are you talking about?" Langa asked, perplexed.

"You better keep your mouth shut, Tramp!" Eric shouted.

"Tramp? You keep on calling me names, Mr. Junkie, but for your information, I had only slept with one man, who happened to be my boyfriend at the time, before you raped me!" Bonelwa retaliated.

"What! He raped you?" Langa said in disbelief, trying to process what he had just heard, "Oh no, no, it can't be!" Langa sat on the edge of his bed, numbed.

"That's right, Langa, your best friend is a junkie and a rapist!" she pressed on.

"You piece of ..." Eric tried to hit Bonelwa, but was intercepted by a hot punch in the face from Langa. Eric fell on the ground with his nose bleeding.

"I can't believe this, Langa. You've chosen this tramp over your lifetime best friend! I hope she is worth it!" Eric cried from the floor.

"You mean, I have chosen a victim over a rapist and a woman basher junkie? Hell yea! And you are not my friend, a man that rapes, verbally abuses and hits a woman, can never be my friend, ever. Get out of my room, you make sick! I don't want to ever see you again. I'm calling the police!" Langa yelled.

"Langa, please don't call the police, they will arrest and deport him; and deep inside, that's what I really want, for him to be beaten up, abused and raped in jail. It is what this piece of crap deserves!" she shouted at the top of her voice.

"But just let him go, one way or the other, he'll get what he deserves. I don't want the police to get involved because I am not ready to face the public humiliation that comes with that, and I don't want my parents to suffer humiliation and be the subject of gossip and pity in my home-town, so please let him go," she requested.

"Okay… but, are you sure? For he surely deserves to rot in jail and taste how it feels to be raped!" Langa disapproved of Bonelwa's decision to let Eric go free, as he looked at Eric with disgust.

"Yes, I am sure," she assured him.

"Okay, it is your call," he agreed. Looking at Eric, he said, "Get out of my room, you piece of crap! And never again come back here or try to contact me; if you ever come near me again, I promise you, I will not be responsible for my actions."

Eric, embarrassed and ashamed, got up from the floor and walked toward the door. As he was about to leave, he turned back and looked at Bonelwa, but she looked at him with disdain and moved her left hand fingers to bid him goodbye. And with a revengeful and wicked smile, she whispered, "It's payback time, loser."

Langa didn't see, or hear, anything she said, as she was standing behind him.

She left Langa's room feeling victorious for successfully taking vengeance on Eric and getting away with it; she patted herself on the back as she walked all the way to her room.

"Did you see his face when his best friend cast him off like dirt? Hahahahha! That was hilarious! I wonder where he went, after being treated like dirt, maybe to sniff coke? Anyway, I don't care, as long he has learned not to treat people like dirt. It is one for me and nil for you, Eric, loser!" she talked to herself on her way to her room.

"Revenge is sweet! Whoever said revenge is bad, he didn't know how to do it properly. I feel great about myself, I feel liberated!" She continued her conversation with herself.

Her victory was short lived when she saw Tau and Zuki kissing each other on the other side of the corridor. Angry and bitter she rushed to her room. At her room she walked to and fro, saying,

"They'll pay, for this is all their fault; they must pay, and that I will make sure of. Oh yes, they will pay the ultimate punishment for betrayal!"

While she was still speaking, her mobile rang, it was a girl from her class, asking if she could borrow her notes for the last two English classes they'd had because she had missed the classes.

"Hi, it's Melissa… how are you doing?"

"Hi, Melissa, I'm okay, and you?"

"I'm a bit stressed, I guess. Are you ready for the test tomorrow? You think you can give me some tips on what you think might be on the test tomorrow?" Melissa asked.

"No, I am not ready for the test tomorrow. I was completely oblivious to it and have no idea what might be on the test, why do you ask?" Bonelwa replied.

"It's just that you always do so well in English, and I thought you could help me out," she replied.

"I am sorry I can't help you, but you can come and get my notes if that would help," she replied.

"Okay cool, I'm coming right away to get them, thanks!"

"So there is a test tomorrow? Why am I not worried? I guess, because I don't care! Besides, I am too cute to study. Yes! That's it! This is my new motto about my education, 'I am too cute to study,'" Bonelwa said to herself. Then she took her black marker and wrote, "I am too cute to study", boldly on an A4 paper and everywhere else that she could write it.

A few moments later, Melissa came by to pick up the notes and went on her way.

CHAPTER SIX

Two weeks later, the University of Cape Town opened its registration for new undergraduate and post-graduate students. Amu, Zuki's younger brother who had recently matriculated, came to submit his application in person. Zuki was glad to have her younger brother with her. After spending the whole day together, Amu could no longer contain his curiosity, so he decided to ask his big sister.

"Where is Bonelwa?" he asked. "You girls are almost inseparable, so spending the whole day with you and not seeing Bonelwa, is a bit unusual for me. So what's going on? Did she move to another university, or what?"

"No, she is still here, but things have changed between us, and we are no longer friends," Zuki replied.

"Why? What happened? You two were so close."

"Yes, we were… but I guess it's part of life; we must just accept it and move on," Zuki brushed off his questions.

"I was looking forward to seeing her."

"I know, little brother. Wait a minute… you still have a crush on her?"

Amu bowed his head, blushed, nodded his head in agreement and said, "Yep, big time!"

"Amu, you must get that out of your mind or heart, wherever it is, and find yourself a girl your age."

"No, Bonelwa is the one for me. Besides, most girls my age cannot hold an intellectual conversation, like the ones I use to have with Bonelwa when she would come see you at home," he protested. "So, what really happened between the two of you?" he asked.

"It's a bit complicated; it is better if you don't know," Zuki responded.

"I think I have the right to know if you ruined my chances with her or not," he insisted.

"What chances? You never had any chances with her; she was too deeply in love with someone to even consider anyone else, let alone you!"

"Ouch! You said she 'was in love with someone', that is great news for me, I can deal with 'was in love', that means she is free and available, right?"

"I don't know, I suppose so."

"What happened, did he cheat on her?"

"Amu, please."

"Did she cheat on him? It can't be. Bonelwa is not that type of girl, I know her. Is she okay?"

"I guess, I must just as well tell you myself."

"Tell me what, Zuki?"

"I stole her boyfriend. My new boyfriend, Tau, was the one she was, or is, in love with."

"You what? How could you do that to your best friend, Zuki?"

"I don't know; I guess I was envious. She kept on telling me how great Tau was and all that they did together; so I was curious and wanted to try Tau myself. But I didn't expect us to fall in love, it was supposed to be just a one-night stand, and Bonelwa wouldn't have known. But Tau fell in love with me and Bonelwa found out. They broke up, and Tau and I are together, but the price I have paid to be with Tau is too high. I've lost my best friend, who was so good to me; she was always there for me," Zuki confessed, almost tearing up. "The worst part, is that I don't even know how she is coping with all of this, because when she found out, she became so violent, I think if she'd had a gun at the time, Tau and I would be history," she continued, her eyes flowing with guilty tears.

"It's okay, Zuki, you can't change what happened. I just hope it was all worth it, and that your relationship with Tau works out for the best."

"I hope so too."

"Give Bonelwa some time. She will eventually forgive you, she is a good person."

"Yes, she is a good person. I just hope, somehow I could make it up to her, so that I may have peace of mind. Even though Tau and I are happy together, when I think about what I have done to her, I question our relationship. I just hope she finds love soon, and forgets about this great evil Tau and I did to her."

"I hope so too. Maybe that is the reason I am here. This is my greatest opportunity yet, I must make my move now, before I regret it for the rest of my life. I must see her tomorrow!" Amu announced.

"No, Amu, I don't think that is a good idea," Zuki protested.

"Zuki, don't you get it? This is my chance, either I make my move now or I'll regret it forever. I must make my move! Tomorrow I will tell her how I really feel about her, and let her decide."

"Okay, just remember, I've warned you."

The following day, Amu waited for Bonelwa on the walkway. When her last class ended, Bonelwa decided to go straight to her room. She passed by Amu, but she didn't recognize him, as her mind was too preoccupied with the terrible pain in her heart. So, she passed him without greeting him. Amu was expecting a warm welcome, as in times past; she was always glad to see and talk to him. After digesting for a moment why she passed him without greeting him, he decided to give her the benefit of the doubt. "Maybe she didn't recognize me," he thought to himself, and ran after her.

"Bonelwa, Bonelwa... wait up!" She turned back to see who was calling her name, and she saw Amu coming her direction.

"Amu, is that you?" she asked.

"In flesh and blood," he replied.

"What are you doing here?"

"I'm just trying to claim my place in this prestigious university!"

"Wow! Look at you, all grown up!"

"Yes, there is a time in a boy's life when he must become a man, and that time has come for me."

After a brief silence, "So, Bonelwa, how are you doing?"

"Not my best year... but I guess I am fine."

"I hope me being here can change your gloomy year into fair sunshine!"

"I know you mean well, Amu, but I doubt that's possible. I don't think anyone can reverse the wrongs that were done to me."

"What about you let me buy you a cup of coffee and we take it from there?"

"Sorry, Amu, but I don't think that's a good idea; it's not you. I would love to have a cup of coffee with you and catch up on old times, while having an intellectual conversation with you, but the truth is that many terrible things have happened and things have changed, I've changed. I am not the person I used to be."

"I totally understand, Bonelwa, no pressure. If you need some time, I'll wait and hope that we can have that elusive cup of coffee; not as Zuki's younger brother, but as a friend."

The mention of Zuki's name stirred up something inside her, bringing to remembrance what she did to her, and looking at her brother, she said, "I am sorry, but I have to go."

She resumed the walk toward her room. Amu came after her and gave her his number, saying, "If you ever need anything, or just want to talk, please don't hesitate to call me."

"Okay, thanks." She took the piece of paper with his number and went to her room.

At her room, she became very agitated. She hated the fact that she had become a charity case, a subject of gossip on campus, and how not one of the people that hurt her had sincerely apologized to her.

"They all will pay. Yes, they will, I will make sure of that. One way or the other, I will make them all pay, and I shall be the last one laughing! They don't know what I am capable of, they should ask Eric!" She said to herself while sitting on her bed, rubbing both hands on her thighs, and thinking about how to make Tau and Zuki feel the pain she had been feeling since she found out about their betrayal.

"Yes! That's it! Very clever... not bad, not bad at all," she exclaimed, as she admired her own wit for coming up with such a "brilliant" plan.

The following day she went to her favorite reading spot in the garden. To her surprise, she found Amu already there, reading a classical novel. She greeted him without making a sound, not wanting to disturb other readers, and she began reading her book.

An hour later, she got up and motioned Amu to follow her, so he gladly closed his book and followed her. When they were away from the reading zone she said, "What about you buying me that cup of coffee that you've promised?"

"Of course, when?"

"What about you fetching me from my room at seven tonight?"

"Sure, I would love that."

"Here is my room number... don't be late. A gentleman must never keep a lady waiting," she handed him the piece of paper with her room number.

"Certainly, Madam."

"Good, I will be expecting you then."

They departed from each other's company and left to prepare themselves for their date. Amu waited until it was safe for him to celebrate.

"Yes!" he said lifting his closed up fist in a celebration fit, "She is mine! I can't wait until I see Zuki's face when I tell her."

At twenty minutes to seven, Amu was outside Bonelwa's room. After waiting for a little while, the two headed to a coffee shop. As they sat there and conversed with each other, it seemed to both of them like the good old days, as if nothing had changed. That is, until

Bonelwa received a wakeup call from her broken heart; and even though Amu's wits were at their best and the conversation was delightful, Bonelwa's heart reminded her of the harsh reality of her life—that her life had changed for the worse and it would never be the same again. The pain in her broken heart would not let her enjoy the delightful moment she was having with Amu. The more they talked about the past, the more the wounds in her heart were opened afresh.

So, in the twinkle of an eye, she turned from Bonelwa, the girl that enjoys fine arts and literature, to the plotting Bonelwa, and for the rest of the outing, she looked at Amu as the brother of her enemy. And she went from genuinely enjoying the conversation, to pretending to enjoy the conversation.

A few moments later, they called it a night, and he walked her to her room and went his way. Amu then told his sister about his success in winning Bonelwa's heart.

The following day he declared his love to Bonelwa and to his surprise she responded positively to his love.

Days and weeks past, and Amu could not be happier; the girl of his dreams was finally his.

Two months later, they were both invited to Tau's graduation ceremony. The cheers and applauses were extremely loud when Tau's name was called out to come and get his diploma. He was the only one of the graduates that day to graduate with a cum laude degree in law.

After the ceremony, Tau invited all his friends to his graduation party, which his parents had organized for him at a nearby hotel.

At the celebration, after the usual speeches were made, Tau was given the platform to say a few words. He began by thanking his parents and friends and everyone that helped him. Then, he called Zuki to come forward to where he was, and Zuki came forward. And then, right in front of everybody, he knelt down, reached into his right pocket, and said, "Zukisa Mgole, will you marry me?" The music stopped playing in the room and everyone hushed; surprised and excited at the same time, everyone waited for Zuki's answer with great anticipation. Tau's parents were also taken off guard. His father looked at his mother with a look that begged the question, "Did you know about this?" and his mother shook her head in a way that said, "I didn't know."

"Yes!" Zuki replied, "Tau Mafoko, I will marry you!"

The room erupted in celebration for them, but some were not happy at all. One of the unhappy ones was Tau's father, as he wanted Tau to spend the first five years of his working life furthering his studies, while establishing himself as a distinguished attorney. His father wanted Tau to one day become Gauteng's Attorney General, and eventually the country's Attorney General. So, he saw Tau's decision as premature and intended to talk him out of it on their way home.

The other person in the room who was definitely not happy, was Bonelwa. She was infuriated by Tau's public proposal to Zuki. She felt as if Zuki was standing in her place and she was the one to whom Tau was supposed to publicly propose.

However, the day was far from over. After the proposal, Tau announced that he had been offered a job at one of the most prestigious law firms in Gauteng, a firm rival to his dad's law firm. The night couldn't get any worse for his dad; he was considering making an excuse to leave the party, but Tau's mother calmed him down.

Then, before he could sit down, Tau dropped the final bomb for the day, "We are having a baby! Zuki is two months pregnant! Zuki and I will be moving to Gauteng in a few weeks and she will finish her studies there. Thank you again for all your support, we really appreciate it."

Tau took Zuki by the hand and led her to their seats.

Tau's father's face told Tau all he needed to know; his father was not at all pleased with all his announcements, but the joy in his mother's face compensated for his father's sour face. Like sugar in bitter coffee.

Bonelwa was fuming at this stage; she was angry, hurt, and disappointed all at once. If she could just wipe away the happiness from the traitors' faces, life would be bearable; she could no longer endure the torturous sight of seeing Tau and Zuki so happy together. She desperately waited for the day that their relationship would collapse, for she always saw Zuki as a loose girl and Tau as a conservative kind of guy, so in her mind, there was no way that their relationship could work. So she was expecting their relationship to last, at most, few months; but seeing Tau proposing to her frenemy, she realized that she had hoped in vain. Disappointed, she went outside to make a call while everybody was busy congratulating the newly engaged couple. She managed to return before Amu could notice that she was gone; and when she saw Amu standing in the queue to congratulate the couple, she joined him and stood behind him. After Amu had congratulated the couple, it was Bonelwa's turn. Zuki was feeling very uncomfortable and Tau was very nervous, but to their surprise,

Bonelwa didn't cause a scene or anything of the kind, she simply said, "Congratulations! You two deserve each other."

Tau and Zuki looked at each other not sure of what to make of her remark, whether they should take it as an insult or just accept it as a compliment. Not wanting to ruin their special day, they decided to take it as a compliment and said, "Thank you."

"You're welcome! Enjoy your happiness while it lasts, and beware of the happiness robbers."

The two gave her no answer, but bowed their heads in shame.

Later that day, when most guests were leaving the party, Bonelwa asked Amu to walk her to the gate of the campus. When they arrived there, she told him, "Go help your sister and be there for her in case she needs you. But make sure you come to my room at nine o'clock sharp, don't be late, I have a great surprise for you. If you are late, you will miss the surprise; remember the rule, 'Never keep...'"

"Never keep a lady waiting," Amu intercepted.

After waiting for a long while, as Tau talked with his parents; Zuki, tired and worried, asked Amu to walk her to her room. She signalled to Tau that she was tired and was leaving to rest; Tau signalled to her that he would meet her in her room, shortly. Zuki agreed, and accompanied by her brother, she left the hotel and headed for campus. By the time they arrived at Zuki's corridor, Tau was right behind them, saying, "Thanks Buddy, I appreciate the help, but I'll take it from here. Go and have fun with... you know who."

"Okay, thanks, Tau. Please look after my sister. I will see you tomorrow or the day after, who knows how busy I will be? Don't wait up!" Amu said, rushing to Bonelwa's room.

It was two minutes to nine when he arrived at Bonelwa's room, and he found the door slightly opened. When he opened the door a bit wider, he saw Bonelwa's red g-string lying on the floor. Excited, he entered the room and found Bonelwa in bed with Langa.

"Bonelwa! How could you do this to me?" Amu cried out. With a broken heart and eyes full of tears, he left the room and went his way, moping, trying to process what he had just seen. Unable to deal with his pain, he went to the only place he could find comfort—his sister's room.

When he got there, Tau and Zuki were busy celebrating, and Zuki wanted to give Tau a special treat. While she was busy unzipping Tau's trousers, Amu knocked on the door.

"Whoever you are, please go away! Otherwise, I will be a very angry man, and you don't want that!" Tau answered the knock on the door.

"It's me, Tau, please open," Amu pleaded in a lamenting and crying voice. Zuki got worried, so she quickly dressed and opened the door.

Amu burst into the room crying, "Bonelwa is having an affair behind my back, I just found her in bed with another guy! How could she do this to me?" he cried out, tears flowing down his distressed face.

"What? Are you sure, Amu? Maybe you went to the wrong room or maybe it is one of her friends with her boyfriend. How can you be so sure that it's her?" Zuki tried to comfort her brother.

"No, Zuki, it is her. I know Bonelwa, and I am sure it's her, I saw them with my own eyes!" he affirmed. "Can I sleep here with you guys? If you don't mind, I don't want to be alone right now."

Zuki looked at Tau, asking for permission. Tau was clearly displeased with Amu's request, so he gave Zuki no answer; Zuki, worried about her brother's well-being and safety, said, "Yes, I guess that would be fine, right Honey?"

Tau looked at her, gave her a forced smile, and said, "Yes, I suppose it's okay."

Their special night turned sour, as a man lamenting his lost love with a box full of tissues to wipe his sad tears away, made the couple sad on his account.

CHAPTER SEVEN

T hat very night while they were all trying to get some sleep, Amu, who was sleeping on the couch, cried with an almost inaudible voice, "I can't... I can't... I can't breathe."

Zuki, who was half asleep, heard it but didn't make much of it.

Amu became restless and called, "Zuki, I can't breathe, I can't breathe!"

"Oh my God! Tau, Amu is having a shortness of breath attack, he suffers from asthma, please call an ambulance," Zuki announced, getting off the bed and rushing to where her brother was laying down.

"Amu, Amu, where is your medication?" she asked in desperation.

"It's..." he tried to talk but the words would not come out.

"Where? Amu, where?" Zuki asked, crying.

"It's... in my room," he softly replied.

"Hello? We have an emergency at the University of Cape Town, please send an ambulance right away, someone who suffers from asthma is having an attack, please hurry!" Tau shouted on the phone on the other side of the room.

A few minutes later the paramedics arrived, and they were directed to Zuki's room. After performing an intervention on the scene, they succeeded in getting Amu to breathe oxygen and stabilized him. He was taken out of the room and led to the ambulance parked outside. By the time they came out, the place was filled with people wondering what had happened, and among the people was Bonelwa.

As they rushed Amu to the hospital, Zuki followed the paramedics crying, while Tau was holding her hand trying to comfort her.

When Bonelwa saw Zuki in great pain, she said to herself, "Now you know how it feels to lose someone that you so dearly love." She went back to her room to celebrate her success.

That was her "brilliant plan"—hurt Amu so deeply that Zuki would feel the pain, and then Tau would be in pain because Zuki was in pain.

That day, when she decided to go out with Amu, her plan was to make Amu fall deeply in love with her and then severely break his heart to get back at Zuki and Tau. In order for her plan to be successful and effective, she had to make Amu think that she was interested in him, and also falling in love with him. So she played her cards very carefully, though at that time she was supposedly Langa's girlfriend, she was crafty in making Amu believe that she had no one at the time. Langa's promising soccer career and his obsession with the game, made it easy for Bonelwa to play a single girl because Langa spent most of his time in practice, traveling, and playing games, which left Bonelwa by herself most of the time and gave her the freedom to spend as much time as she could with Amu.

When she saw Tau so happily proposing to Zuki, the two of them glowing with happiness, with a baby on the way and plans to move to Gauteng together, it was all too perfect— except that she was the one who should be Tau's fiancée, not Zuki.

Enraged she went out, called Langa, and made arrangements for the two of them that night; then she asked Amu to come over at the time she would make sure that she would be in bed with Langa. Having trained Amu to be on time, every time, she knew he would be there in time to find them together in bed. So she intentionally left the door of her room open, to give Amu easy access, and placed her red g-string right in front of the door to increase his excitement— and make the disappointment even greater. Everything worked out just as she had planned, though she was a bit worried about Amu's well-being. However, seeing the pain on Zuki's face, superseded her concerns about Amu.

"Revenge, sweet revenge. The victory belongs to the one who laughs last. But I am not yet through with you, Zuki and Tau. You will pay for all that you have done to me, the pain and humiliation you put me through, I shall retaliate six times more. You've messed with the wrong girl!" she said to herself, while celebrating her first victory in bringing pain to Tau's and Zuki's hearts.

At the hospital, Amu was taken to an emergency unit. After some preliminary tests, the doctor attending to him came out; he found Zuki anxiously waiting for an update about her brother's well-being.

"Ms. Mgole?" the doctor asked Zuki, trying to make sure that he was talking to the right person.

"Yes, Doctor, how is my brother doing?" Zuki responded, getting up.

"I am Dr. Petersen, your brother is stable for now, but I must say, it is a miracle that he is alive. It was a very timely response by you, calling the paramedics when you did, a few hours later and he would have died. It seems a very stressful situation triggered the asthma attack causing him to go into cardiac arrest, which shut down his lungs, which is why he could not breathe. If he had been alone, he would have died." the doctor reported.

Zuki looked at Tau in distress, and then asked the doctor, "Can we see him?"

"Yes you can, but please keep it brief, he needs to rest," the doctor gave them permission.

"Yes, Doctor, thank you!" Zuki said, gratefully.

After seeing her brother, Zuki called her mother to notify her of the situation. Her mother wanted to get on the next flight and come to Cape Town, but Zuki convinced her that there was no need, her mother reluctantly agreed.

Seeing her brother plugged into all those tubes and equipment, Zuki didn't want to leave the hospital, so she returned to the ward and asked the nurse if she could stay until her brother woke up.

"I don't want him to panic when he wakes up and see only strange faces. I believe if he sees me when he wakes up, he will be at ease," Zuki told the nurse.

"Okay, but only one of you can stay," the nurse conceded.

Zuki asked Tau to go back to campus and rest. Tau was not very happy leaving his pregnant fiancée behind to sleep on a chair, but there was not much he could do. He departed from the hospital and went back to the campus.

Early in the morning, Amu woke up and saw Zuki sleeping on the chair, leaning her head on his bed.

"Zuki…" he called.

Zuki was fast asleep. She had spent the whole night awake and finally fell asleep only an hour before he woke up. When he heard her snoring, Amu lifted his left hand and brushed her hair and gently woke her up.

"Hey, I am very sorry for everything, I didn't mean to cause all this trouble."

"It's okay Amu, please rest, I'm right here."

"Please go rest, I'm fine now. If you stay here, you'll worry me; besides, I'm in very capable hands."

"No, Amu, please don't worry about me. I'm fine, please rest."

"Zuki, please go rest, you are pregnant and you need proper rest—otherwise you will stress me out."

"Okay, I'm going, but I will come back later, okay?"

"Okay. Hey, thanks for everything, you saved my life...thank you!"

"Don't mention it, that's what big sisters are for. Please rest, I will see you later."

"Okay."

When she arrived on campus, she decided to pay Bonelwa a visit. Before she could knock on the door, the door was opened, Bonelwa was on her way to class.

"Hi, Bonelwa."

"Hi!"

"We need to talk."

"Can we talk some other time, I'm on my way to class."

"This won't take long... can I come in?"

"Be my guest, but you are coming in at your own risk."

"Okay," Zuki said, scared.

She took courage and entered Bonelwa's room.

"Bonelwa, please hear me out. I'm very sorry for what I have done to you, please forgive me. You have every right to be angry and hate me and Tau. If it was possible to reverse it, I would, but I can't. But, Amu didn't do anything to you, why make him pay for my sins? He almost died! If you want to punish me and Tau, go ahead, we deserve it, but Amu is innocent… please leave my brother out of this."

"Zuki, it is too late for you to apologize. Can you fix my broken heart? If you can undo all the hurt and pain that you put me through, and restore my heart the way it was before your betrayal, I will gladly accept your apology and forgive you—but if you can't do that, you are wasting your time. As for Amu, he is collateral damage. In war, innocent people die. But he is not innocent, he is your brother—that makes him guilty, and so is everyone that you love. One way or another, you will all pay—that I will make sure of!"

"Bonelwa, please leave the people I love alone. What do you want me to do?"

"Zuki, if you can pick up all the shattered pieces of my broken heart and make it whole again, I will leave you, and the people you love, alone. But if you can't, I will be coming after you, Tau, and everyone and everything that you love. I won't rest until I'm satisfied… and I am not easily satisfied."

"Bonelwa, please…"

"Zuki, if you can't fix my heart and make it whole again, you are wasting my time. Anyway, I need to go, I'm going to be late."

Zuki left Bonelwa's room feeling frightened and pitiful at the same time. It was as if the Bonelwa she knew was dead, and the one she talked to was a living corpse. She went straight to Tau's room and told him everything Bonelwa told her, including the threats that she made. Tau became exceedingly worried after hearing it and wanted to leave for Gauteng as soon as possible.

CHAPTER EIGHT

A few days later, Amu was discharged from the hospital, with a stern warning by the doctor to avoid, at all cost, anything or anyone that may cause him to stress—if he wanted to live. Taking the doctor's warning very seriously, he avoided Bonelwa at all costs and restrained himself from going anywhere he might bump into her.

Weeks passed, the time for Tau's and Zuki's departure arrived. After getting all the documents they needed for Zuki to continue her studies, they were set to fly to Gauteng. The cab arrived and, accompanied by Amu, they headed to the airport.

At the airport, Zuki seemed worried while they waited to take the flight.

"What's wrong, Zuki? Why do you look so sad when you are supposed to be excited?" Amu asked.

"I am worried about you, Amu. I don't know if leaving you alone is a wise decision on my part, if something happens to you, I will never forgive myself."

"Relax, Zuki, nothing will happen to me. I am a big boy now, I can look after myself."

"I know. Please promise me that you will not go after her again."

"I promise; besides, I don't want to die because of a girl."

"Okay, take care, Amu. I will see you at the wedding."

"I will, Zuki, and thank you for everything. You always put me first, and I appreciate it, but it's time for you to put Zuki first. Please live your life to the fullest and don't worry about me or anyone else. We'll be fine, this is your time, Zuki, live it."

"I will, thank you, bye."

"Bye, Zuki."

Tau, who was standing by to give the siblings some time alone to talk to each other, came closer and stretched out his right hand to say goodbye to Amu.

Amu hugged him and said, "Please take good care of my sister."

"Don't worry Bro, I got this."

"I'll see you at the wedding."

"Yes, please look after yourself, you scared us. Please don't let it happen again."

"I won't, I will do my best to follow the doc's instructions; I still want to play with my nephew or niece."

"That's right! But let's hope it's a nephew."

"Okay, that would be cool. Bye, Tau, thank you for everything."

"Bye, Amu."

Tau and Zuki boarded the plane. Amu waited until they took off, and returned to campus.

Bonelwa, who was spying on them all along when they left for the airport, got a dose of reality when she saw Amu returning the campus, alone. Tau and Zuki were now out of her reach.

"It is not over yet, Zuki; you can run, but you can't hide," she said to herself.

The following day, she started her research to locate the law firm where Tau would be working. After getting the exact location of the firm, she started hunting for a job in the surrounding areas. To her astonishment, a bank located near the firm was advertising for intern opportunities for their customer care department; the money they were offering to pay, was not that great, but it was enough to cover all her basic needs. So, she decided to apply for the job, and to her delight, she was called to come the following week for an interview. Excited, she asked the campus' office for her academic transcript, so that she may continue her studies in Gauteng. The lady that called her from the bank's human resources, hinted that the interview was just a formality, and that she should come ready to start immediately.

The following week, Bonelwa took all her belongings and headed to the airport. She didn't tell anyone that she was leaving, not even her parents, who were oblivious to all that she was going through. She didn't want to disappoint the high expectations and high standards that her family tried so hard to live by.

She arrived in Gauteng, the day before the interview was scheduled. The day after, she was at the bank for the interview where she exceeded the expectations of the interviewer; she was very good in communication, English being her major, and she was asked to start that very same day. She gladly accepted.

After seven days of induction to their systems, she was placed in the department where she would be working. Everything fell into place, just as she had envisioned.

After a month of spying outside Tau's firm, from a restaurant opposite the firm, there was no sign of Tau. Disappointed, she returned to the bank, doubting if she had the right address.

Tired and disillusioned with her plan of revenge, she took her lunch, but instead of sitting where she always sat, facing the entrance of the firm, she decided to sit at a back booth, facing the wall. After ordering, while she ate her lunch, she heard Tau's voice talking with his older brother about the wedding arrangements.

Tshepo, Tau's older brother, had been recently released from a mental institution. His divorce from his nine-year marriage to his ex-wife was very messy, after he found her in bed with his boss. He didn't take it well, and it almost drove him insane.

"Tshepo, how are you holding up?" Tau asked.

"Honestly, I'm trying to take one day at the time," he replied.

"Are you seeing anyone yet?"

"Not yet... I guess, I am afraid of getting hurt again."

"Take all the time you need, there is no need to rush into a relationship and regret it later."

"Yes, thanks Buddy. That is why I don't think I am the right person to be your best man, I don't want to spoil your wedding day, Tau. Maybe you should get a more suitable person."

"Tshepo, look at me, you are my big brother and best friend. Who else could be more suitable than you?"

"Okay, I think you're right, I'll do it."

"Of course I'm right. Don't worry, Tshepo, it will all work out just fine. Do you have a date already?"

"Nope, do I have to have one?"

"No, I was just asking... besides, there will be plenty of single ladies there, who knows, maybe your true soul mate will be there."

"I doubt that, Tau."

"Anyway, we only have one month to get all that is needed; if you need anything, just give me a shout."

"Okay, Buddy, thank you for choosing me, I really appreciate it."

"No problem. I have to rush back to the office, but don't forget about the family dinner we are having tonight at eight o'clock."

"Oh, is it tonight? Thanks for reminding me, I almost forgot. I'll see you later, Buddy."

Bonelwa could not believe her good fortune as she saw them walking out of the restaurant. Her eyes followed Tau until he entered the firm's building opposite the restaurant. Her spirit of revenge was revived after seeing Tau. She sat there thinking and planning on how to avenge herself best.

Her lunch break was over, she returned to the bank in a very good mood.

The next day, on her lunch break, she stood at a distance waiting for Tau to come out. He came out a few minutes later with his brother and three other guys, and they headed to a shop not far from the firm. Bonelwa followed them at a distance until they entered a clothing shop. She saw them fitting the suits and being helped with the measurements for adjustments. When she saw Tau wearing his wedding suit, she remembered how she used to dream about having her dream wedding with Tau. Seeing Tau wearing the suit style and colour that she always told Zuki about, was too painful for her to bear. Zuki didn't just steal her man, she stole her dream also. She went her way crying—she couldn't take it anymore.

She took her heels off and carried them in her hand, the pain in her heart made them too straining to walk on. She kept on walking, without knowing where she was going, until she found herself sitting on a bench in a park crying bitter tears. She didn't care who was passing by, her sorrowful heart could no longer hold back the pain, so she let her deep hurt flow freely through her tears.

By the time she came to her senses, she was an hour late for work. She quickly wiped her tears and ran back to the bank, without ever having lunch. She sighed in relief, when she arrived at the bank and noticed that her supervisor was not there. She quickly got to her desk and buried herself in her work, trying to make up for the lost hour, while trying to deal with her pain at the same time.

CHAPTER NINE

The month passed quickly, and the wedding day had arrived. All was set for the big day, no cost was spared in any way; it was a wedding fit for a princess. From a five-star venue, décor, and chefs, to high profile guests—it was a day to be remembered.

Though adamant at first, Tau's father, convinced by his wife, finally warmed up to the idea of having his first grandchild. And because he did not want his grandchild to be born out of wedlock, he advised Tau and Zuki to get married as soon as possible and offered to pay for everything.

They agreed and took his advice. And from that day, he set the ball rolling to give his son the best wedding possible.

The venue was a five-star majestic lounge with gorgeous grandeur, at The View Boutique Hotel, in Auckland Park, Johannesburg.

The theme colour was creamy white and ocean blue with a dash of gold.

The matrimonial ceremony was set at The View's beautiful landscaped garden, staged with a beautiful white wedding gazebo.

The reception was to take place inside The View's most prestigious lounge.

At last, after all the last minute final touches, the hour for the proceedings had arrived. All was set, the groom was in his position, and the groomsmen and bridesmaids were in their respective positions. Then, the famous pianist, hit the chords sounding the traditional bridal chorus, "Here Comes the Bride", and all were asked to rise, as Zuki, accompanied by her father, marched on the red carpet to the gazebo.

Then the minister officiating the wedding asked all to sit. After having everyone seated, he began the ceremony with an introduction for the purpose of their gathering, and carried on officiating the ceremony.

After the ceremony, the couple, groomsmen, and bridesmaids were then directed to take photos, while the rest of the guests were invited to partake in some five-star cocktails and enjoy the expansive lush gardens.

When the photo session ended, the guests were escorted to the magnificent reception venue and seated according to the arrangement.

A few moments later, the newlyweds, groomsmen and bridesmaids made their grand entrance into the reception lounge, with the DJ introducing the newlyweds' grand entrance:

"Ladies and Gentlemen, please give a warm welcoming applause to Mr. and Mrs. Mafoko!"

The guests rose and clapped their hands, while the couple marched to the main table, where parents from both sides were already seated; and they joined them by sitting according to the prescribed arrangement.

After some announcements were made, dinner was served, to the delight of many guests, who could not wait to get a taste of the magnificent dishes. The DJ played some soft music in the background, while the guests ate. He played some classics for the old and the young, and everyone enjoyed his selections.

Dinner ended, and announcements, along with some speeches (some short and some long), were made, which led some of the young guests to get bored; they were eagerly waiting for the first dance to get the party started.

"Finally!" was the sigh of relief from some guests when the first dance was announced. Lights were dimmed, the DJ pressed play, and out of the speakers came: "Better Together," by Jack Johnson.

Tau took Zuki into his arms and led her through their first dance as a married couple, as the song's lyrics played out:

"It's not always easy… Sometimes life can be deceiving… I'll tell you one thing, it's always better when we're together…"

The lyrics rang so true to their situation. Zuki, looked into Tau's eyes and said, "Our love may be stolen, but it's real… truly, 'it's always better when we're together.'"

Tau locked his eyes with Zuki and replied, "I love you and I would not trade this very moment to be with someone else. Zuki, you are the only one for me."

"Thank you, Honey. It means a lot hearing you saying these words to me. Please promise me one thing…"

"Sure, what is it?"

"Please promise me that you will never cease to say these words I have just heard, for the rest of our lives…especially, after I give birth and start getting old."

"I promise; I only have eyes for you."

Their sweet conversation progressed until the song was almost over, and that is when the guests joined them in a romantic dance.

Just as the song was ending, and dancing partners were about to part ways, the DJ faded in, "We Belong Together", by Mariah Carey, and no one left the dance floor. Then to round it up, he played "On Bended Knee", by Boyz II Men.

Their dance was interrupted when Zuki's Dad asked to dance with his daughter. Tau gladly made way for his father-in-law, left them dancing, and went to sit at his table.

After only a few seconds seated, his brother, Tshepo, excitedly grabbed him from behind and said, "Come on, Dude, I want you to meet someone very special to me."

"Okay, that's great! I am happy for you, Tshepo..."

"Tau, I know it's very soon to tell, but she might just be the one!"

"Okay, now I really want to meet her. Let's go and meet 'the one' where is she?"

"Just follow me and you'll meet her."

The two headed through the crowded dance floor until they arrived next to the wall where some people were seated watching people dancing.

Tshepo tapped her on her shoulder saying, "Tau, meet Amanda; and Amanda, meet my brother Tau."

She turned around and said, "Hi Tau, it is a pleasure meeting you."

"Hi Amanda... the pleasure is all mine," Tau replied, staggered.

Tshepo's phone rang, it was his mother asking him to come to the main table, she needed his assistance.

"I have to go, my mother is calling me. I'll leave you two to get to know each other better," Tshepo said, kissing Amanda. Then said,

"You are in safe hands, Baby. I'll be right back," and he left them alone.

"Bonelwa, what are doing here?" Tau angrily whispered.

"Your brother invited me."

"Really, just like that?"

"Yes, just like that, Tau. If you have any problem with that, take it up with your brother."

"Why the fake name and dyed short hair?"

"It is not a fake name, it is my middle name! As for my hair, I guess I needed a fresh start, do you like it?"

"How did you guys meet anyway? Did you guys meet online or what? A few weeks back, he was single. I know that because, he told me… and now he shows up with you. What is really going on, Bonelwa?"

"Please call me Amanda, Bonelwa died—and you killed her! We did not meet online. Two weeks ago, we bumped into each other at the door of the Nando's, where I usually eat my lunch. We were both busy texting on our phones without looking at where we were going, so we literally bumped into each other. And to make it up to me, he asked if he could buy me lunch, and I said, yes. We had lunch together that day, and let's just say, that we clicked. We have been seeing each other ever since."

"So, let me just get this straight, are you saying that you work here in Johannesburg?"

"Yes, that is right; I work at the bank in Rivonia, next to the Nando's, where we met."

"Nando's at Rivonia? Wow! That's very convenient for you, isn't it? One minute we leave you in Cape Town, the next you are working next to the firm where I work; that was a bit too fast, don't you think? And a bit too coincidental for me. I am beginning to think that you are stalking me."

"You can think whatever you want, that is none of my business. And yes, things are happening very fast these days. I lost my first boyfriend in four days, can you believe that? Four days, that is all it took for some loose girl to steal the man that I loved!"

Tau's pricked conscience left him without words.

Zuki returned to their table and asked where Tau was. Tshepo, who was busy helping his mother, told her where to find him.

She saw Tau talking to a woman, not wanting to take any chances, she rushed there to get her husband and bring him back to her side. When she got closer, she recognized Bonelwa from afar.

"Oh, hell no!" she exclaimed, as she stood and watched her frenemy talking with Tau.

Worried, she rushed to where they were.

"You just couldn't resist, could you?" Zuki shouted at Bonelwa.

"Don't flatter yourself, Ms. Loose Girl; I am trying to be nice and civil, but if you want me to change, and act differently, I can also do that for you, and tell everyone in here, who you really are." Bonelwa shouted.

"There is no need for that," Tau intercepted.

Looking at his wife, he said, "Baby, please let me handle this. Please go back to our table and wait for me there."

"No way! There is just no way that I will leave you alone with her—who knows what she is capable of?"

The music was loud, and most people could not hear them talking, but Zuki's and Bonelwa's voices were getting louder with each exchange of words. Fearing someone might hear their quarrel, Tau suggested that they all go talk somewhere private.

"Please follow me," he pleaded with them.

"Okay, Baby you are right, I don't want our wedding night to be ruined," Zuki said, giving Bonelwa a despising look and following her husband. Bonelwa followed right after her.

With the assistance of the hotel manager, Tau found a small chamber where the three of them could have a private conversation.

After closing the door behind them, Tau, mentally drained, asked, "Bonelwa, what are you really doing here?"

"Yes! Good question, what are you doing here?" Zuki added.

"Baby, please…" Tau asked Zuki to let him handle it.

"Thank you for shushing Ms. Loose Girl, she can be annoying sometimes—to be fair, most of the time," Bonelwa replied sarcastically.

Then, looking at Tau, she said, "I told you not to call me that again, this is your last warning! Are you going to ask me the same thing over and over again? For the last time, and please hear this time because I am not going to repeat myself again, I met Tshepo two weeks back and we started going out. That is when he told me about him being a best man in his younger brother's wedding, and asked me if I would like to go with him, so I said, yes. But as he continued to speak about you guys, I realized that it was your wedding that he wanted to take me to. That is when I started making excuses for me not to come, but he kept on pestering me and he would not take no for an answer. So, I agreed to come, and today he literally dragged me here, to parade me as his precious trophy among his family and friends, to boost his male ego. And if he would not have tried to impress his little brother, by introducing us to each other, I would have left this fake wedding without you knowing that I was here."

"Fake wedding?" Zuki asked, angry.

"Yes, why is our wedding fake?" Tau asked, perplexed.

"Ask Ms. Loose Girl here, she should tell you," Bonelwa said.

"Tell him what? There is nothing to tell," Zuki asked, irritated.

"Yes, tell me what?" Tau asked.

"So, you don't want to tell him? Okay, I will do the honours," Bonelwa said.

"Bonelwa, what are talking about?" Tau asked.

"See, your precious Slut here, didn't just steal you from me, she also stole my dream wedding!" Bonelwa shouted.

"What do you mean, she stole your dream wedding? What is she talking about, Baby?" Tau asked.

"I don't know, Tau!" Zuki shrieked in shame.

"You don't know? Okay, let me refresh your memory. All of this is my idea. The suit you are wearing is my idea, the wedding dress she is wearing and how she is looking is also my idea; except the pregnancy, I wouldn't trap a man with a child, and I definitely wouldn't want to get married pregnant. This venue is also my idea; the gazebo and the theme colours, the dishes, the décor, the first dance song, it is all my idea. At the ceremony, when the minister asked, 'If there is anyone here who knows a just cause why they should not lawfully be joined in marriage, I implore you to speak now, or forever hold your peace.' I promise you, I almost got up and told everyone what phonies you really are... but I decided to let it go, for you two deserve each other. See, Mr. Cheater, your wedding is a sham and a mockery. This is my dream wedding, without me being in it as the bride; come to think of it, I have all the right to be here, because if it were not for me, you would not be here," Bonelwa told Tau.

Tau looked at Zuki in disbelief, and with a sad face, he asked, "Is it true Baby? That this is all her idea? Please tell me it's not true…"

"Who cares whether it is true or not, Tau? Ms. Envious must just accept that you chose me over her and get a new dream and move on with her life!" Zuki retorted.

"Oh no, it is true," Tau said, disappointed.

After a few moments of silence Tau said, "Bonelwa, I am very sorry that I cheated on you and broke your heart, and that Zuki stole all your ideas of your dream wedding. Please let it go and move on."

"Just like that? Let it go and move on. It's easy for you to stand there and say those words; you are not the one that has been stabbed in the heart with the knife of betrayal!" Bonelwa shouted.

"Bonelwa, what do you want from us? What must we do for you to leave us alone?" Tau asked.

"I don't want anything from you, except that you suffer for what you have done to me. What must you do for me to leave you alone? Let me see… Okay, I need you to do three things for me and, if you do them, I promise to leave you and your slut alone and you don't ever have to see my face again," Bonelwa retorted.

"Okay, just name them and we will do them," Tau agreed.

"One, you must restore my heart to the way it was, before you broke it. Two, you must restore my virginity. And three, you must take away all the pain and humiliation I have had to endure, since we broke up. You do those three things and I will leave you alone. But, if you fail to do them, I promise you Tau, I will dump Tshepo and hurt him so deeply, that it will make what his ex-wife did to him, look like a picnic. I will hurt him so badly, that it will drive him really insane this time. Who knows what he will do this time, maybe commit suicide? I don't know, only time will tell," Bonelwa demanded.

"Bonelwa, please leave my brother out of this; it is me and Zuki that did you wrong, my brother didn't do anything wrong to you," Tau pleaded.

"Tau, you should've thought about it before you trampled on my gentle, loyal and faithful heart; you have created a monster, Tau, and now you have to deal with it," Bonelwa retorted.

"Bonelwa, please..." Tau begged.

"Three things, Tau; that is all I am asking. You do them, and you can enjoy your fake marriage with your slut here in peace. By the way, you must do them in three days."

She then looked at her watch and said, "Oops! The countdown has begun a few seconds ago—three days, Tau. I need to go, Tshepo might be looking for me."

Just as she was going out, Tshepo came into the room.

"There you are, I've been looking all over for you," Tshepo said.

"I am right here, Honey," Bonelwa retorted.

Seeing Tau and Zuki looking down, Tshepo asked, "What's going on here?"

"Nothing is going on, Honey. I was just having a delightful conversation with the newlyweds, that's all. Let's go back to the party, I don't want to miss anything," Bonelwa responded.

"Okay, Luv," Tshepo agreed.

As they were leaving the room, Bonelwa showed them three fingers, signifying that they had three days.

The two left the room and went back to the party, leaving behind the bride and groom pondering what to do.

"Maybe we should get a restraining order against her," Zuki suggested.

"I don't think that is a good idea right now, it would only make her angrier than she already is," Tau disagreed.

"What should we do then? We can't live the rest of our lives watching over our shoulders," Zuki suggested.

"I agree, but right now what we need to do is to go in there and celebrate our wedding with our families and friends, that is what we need to do," Tau said.

"Yes, I agree. Let us not give her the satisfaction of ruining our wedding night by being sad," Zuki agreed.

They held hands, left the room and went back to the reception lounge, and sat at their table. They found Bonelwa talking with Tau's mother next to the table. Their conversation seemed to be a delightful one, as they both kept on laughing out loud, to the displeasure of Zuki, who was desperate to hear what was so funny that kept them laughing. Tau sat there trying to digest the idea that his perfect wedding was all Bonelwa's idea. And so they spent the rest of the reception, worrying that Bonelwa might say or do something wrong to ruin their wedding party.

CHAPTER TEN

Two days later, Tau and Zuki travelled to Mauritius for their honeymoon.

Four days after the wedding, as promised, Bonelwa sent an insensitive heart-breaking SMS to Tshepo, saying:

"Hi, Tshepo, you are a good guy, but I need more than just a good guy, I need a real man that can satisfy me. I need a man that can make me feel like a woman. Unfortunately, you cannot satisfy a woman, at least not me. When I am with you, you always leave me hanging and unsatisfied. It was fun being with you, but your little thing spoils all the fun. So we have to stop seeing each other; I need to find myself a real man. It is over between us, please don't call, or text me, or come to my place. Bye."

Tshepo read and reread the text message several times. He tried to call Bonelwa, but she was not picking up his calls, and that hit his fragile self-esteem hard.

Devastated, his male ego severely bruised, Tshepo got into the nearest bar, and drowned his pain in the bottle until he had to be chased from the bar. Once pushed out of the bar by security, Tshepo started having suicidal thoughts and wished death upon himself; he couldn't take the shame and humiliation any longer. So, he jumped into a busy road with fast cars and motorcycles passing by; he was missed by two cars and then, boom! He was hit by a speeding motorcycle. The impact made his head hit the pavement, causing his head to bleed.

Shortly after that, the paramedics and firemen arrived at the scene and rushed him to the hospital. His parents were notified and they rushed to the hospital. When they arrived, they found him on life support. His mother started crying, fearing the worst. His father went out and called Tau and told him that Tshepo was on life support, and they didn't know whether he would make it or not.

Tau and Zuki packed their bags and immediately returned to Johannesburg. Tau asked the cab driver to drop them at the hospital where Tshepo was.

He found his mother crying next to his brother, with his father trying to comfort her. He joined them and gazed at his emotionless brother, helplessly lying there, and started crying.

Then, wiping his tears, he looked at his dad and asked softly, "What happened?" His dad shrugged his shoulders and said, "We don't really know; all we were told is that he was hit by a speeding motorcycle."

A few hours later, his mother asked Tau to take Zuki home to rest.

"We will keep you posted. If there are any changes, we will let you know right away."

"Okay, Mom," Tau agreed.

They left the room and went on their way. At the lift, Zuki, who hesitated all along, finally decided to ask, "Do you think she did it?"

"I don't know, Zuki!" He shouted, frustrated.

"Tau, chill out, I was just asking a question—you don't have to take it out on me!"

"I am sorry, Baby, I didn't mean to. It's just, he was doing so well and his life was coming together, and now because of me, he is on life-support and he might just die," he said tearing up.

Zuki tried to comfort him; she held him and said, "It's not your fault. Don't beat yourself up, it's going to be fine."

The following day, on their way to the hospital, Zuki suggested that Tau does an investigation to determine whether Bonelwa had anything to do with it. Tau agreed to investigate the incident that led to Tshepo being on life-support.

At the hospital, Tau requested his brother's personal belongings, and it was all given to him. He went through his brother's stuff trying to find a clue about what had led him near to death.

He checked his phone and saw that the last person he called was Bonelwa.

He took the liberty to read his messages and he read the text message Bonelwa sent him. He put his lawyer skills to work and put the pieces together and came to the astonishing conclusion that his brother wanted to commit suicide.

He left the hospital at twelve o'clock, went to the bank where she was working, and waited a few minutes for her to come out for her lunch break.

Bonelwa saw him as she came out, went straight to him and nervously asked, "What are you doing here, Tau?"

"I just wanted to give you the good news in person. Congratulations, you have won."

"I have won what?"

"You have won the game of playing with people's lives. My brother is on life-support as we speak and he might not make it, so congratulations!"

"I am sorry to hear that, but I've warned you; perhaps next time you should take my warnings very seriously."

"I saw the text message you sent him on the day of the incident. I just wanted to tell you in person, that it has worked. You have succeeded in driving him insane, as you promised. But remember, if he dies, his blood will be on your hands!"

"Whatever you say, Tau. For me he is just a casualty; in a war, innocent people are bound to die. Now if you will excuse me, I am starving and I need to grab something to eat."

"Okay! Go ahead and enjoy your triumph… I hope it lasts forever!"

They departed from each other.

At the restaurant while she was eating, she thought about Tshepo's attempted suicide and her conscience pricked her. She questioned her actions and asked herself if it was worth it to push Tshepo to attempt suicide.

Her lunch break was over and she returned to the bank with a heavy heart.

At the hospital, Tau asked Zuki to go with him to the coffee shop inside the hospital. There he told her where he had gone, and notified her that he was considering taking legal action against Bonelwa;

asking the court to issue a restraining order against her. Zuki agreed and fully supported her husband.

"There is only one thing we must consider, if we forge ahead and take legal action against her…" Tau cautioned.

"Which is?" Zuki asked.

"We must tell my parents everything, and I mean everything, so that they are not surprised by anything in court."

"I am not sure about telling them everything, Tau. What if your parents resent me after we tell them everything?"

"I guess that is a risk that we have to take. Besides, in court, there will be no holding back of anything, so it is better if they hear it from us; that way, we will not seem to be defending ourselves, when the time comes."

"Okay, let's do it then."

They returned to the room and asked his parents to join them for a cup of coffee and a serious conversation. So they all went to the coffee shop and Tau and Zuki told them about everything.

His father got very upset when he heard that his son might die because of a revengeful girl. He told Tau to prepare the case and get ready for court. Tau agreed.

"Let us sue this girl and put her where she truly belongs—in prison! She is messing with the wrong family," the old man said, fuming.

CHAPTER ELEVEN

Tension was running high, and the Mafoko family was thinking with their wounded hearts, not with their heads. As they sat there talking about revenge, Mrs. Mafoko, Tau's mother, did not agree with their plotting and tried to talk them out of it, but they would not listen; pain shut their ears to reason. So they went ahead with their plan of revenge, but they did it behind Mrs. Mafoko's back because she would not approve of any of their plans.

They spent seven days plotting how to get back at Bonelwa. Tau's dad got hold of all his "trusted people" and put them in place. On the eighth day, a Monday, they were ready to strike back at Bonelwa with their plan. Two police officers were dispatched to the bank; they waited outside until it was midday, when the bank was packed with people, and they leaked the arrest to media. At quarter past twelve, the two police officers entered the bank and asked for Bonelwa. When she came out, the leading officer read her rights saying:

"Bonelwa Amanda Hlazo, you are under arrest for conspiring against the life of Mr. Tshepo Andrew Mafoko. You have the right to remain silent. Anything you say can and will be used against you in a court of law. You have the right to an attorney. If you cannot afford an attorney, one will be appointed for you."

They handcuffed her in front of her co-workers and customers and led her out, escorted by the two officers. When they came out, the TV cameras and newspapers' photographers were waiting for them and her arrest was broadcasted live. She couldn't even hide her face, because they intentionally handcuffed her hands behind her back so that she would not be able to cover her face.

Ashamed and humiliated, Bonelwa was taken to the back seat of a police van and driven to the nearest police station to be questioned.

The two cops that arrested her took charge of the interrogation. They were aiming to get a confession that she had intentionally conspired against Tshepo's life, to make it an easy case for the judge. They even promised her a lower sentence, if she confessed. But Bonelwa used her right to remain silent and spoke not a word. She was enraged inside. The public humiliation they put her through was eating her up, and she knew herself well enough to know not to open her mouth when she was angry. As much as she wanted to give these two cops a piece of her mind for the way they treated her, she decided not to, for she knew that would only make her situation worse. So she kept her mouth shut. They made her many promises, which didn't work, and when they saw that promises were not working, they switched to threats, which also didn't work.

Tired and confused, her brain stopped functioning as she went through the process of being booked; she was fingerprinted, photographed and put in a holding cell at the police station. The two arresting officers didn't want her to have her initial appearance without first securing a confession to the charges.

She was put in a holding cell to wait for her initial appearance the next day.

Early in the morning, she was taken to court to appear before a judge.

She felt intimidated by the court environment and security forces that were in place. It all became very real to her when she saw real male and female criminals being brought in and out of the various courtrooms.

Finally, it was her turn to appear before the judge. She was terrified of the man sitting in the judge's seat; he looked merciless and uncaring.

The charges against her were read to her before the judge and the judge informed her of all her rights; since she didn't have a lawyer, one was appointed for her. The judge decided to allow her to be released on bail. However, Mr. Mafoko, using his unconventional methods in an attempt to avoid any temporary release, made sure her bail was set at fifteen thousand rands, which was way too much for a person like her. Bonelwa could not afford to pay her bail. Therefore, she was put in a holding cell to wait for her trial which was set for twenty-one days later.

She was told she had the right to make one phone call only. So she sat in her cell thinking about where she should get that kind of money, and whom she should call to help her, but there was no one in Johannesburg that she knew well enough that she could call for help. She wanted to call her parents but she just couldn't bring herself to do it.

She fell asleep, out of sorrow, on the uncomfortable stone bed.

At five 'til noon, her cell was opened and she was awakened by the shout of a female police officer, "Ms. Hlazo, you are free to go. Get all your belongings on your way out."

She didn't waste time in asking the officer what happened, or why she was now free to go; she was just glad she could go home. When she got to where she was to get her belongings, the clerk informed her that someone had paid her bail and left a sealed envelope for her. He handed her all of her belongings, along with the sealed envelope.

Curious and nervous at the same time, she opened the envelope while she rode back home on a bus. There was a note inside that read as follows:

"Hi, Bonelwa, you don't know me but you can call me, The Associate.

It seems that you have pissed off some very powerful people in this town. They are ready to fry you alive and send you to prison to teach you a lesson, and they will succeed, unless you do exactly as I tell you.

I believe you have appeared in court this morning, for your initial appearance, and the judge informed you of your legal rights and what you should do. Most likely, because you cannot afford a lawyer, I presume the judge has advised you to request one appointed by the court.

Now, here is my advice to you… you must not use a state appointed lawyer during your trial, and please do not contact a private attorney. If you take my advice, I will guide you through your trial, making sure you don't condemn yourself, and you will have a better chance of walking away from this free. But, if you reject my advice, this will be our last conversation.

There are two things you should know: first, the court appointed lawyer that represented you today, is with them, that is why he never argued for a lesser bail. Second, judging by the high bail that the judge put as a condition of your temporary release, it is more likely, that he is also with them.

The best chance you have of walking away free from these charges, is to put your freedom in your own hands. No one values, or desires to keep your freedom at any cost, like you do.

Therefore, you must represent yourself during the trial. You will be both the defendant, and your own 'lawyer', at the same time. Don't worry, though it is a difficult thing to do, it is doable and I will be guiding you every step of the way. All you have to do is to follow my instructions, do exactly as I say, and you will be fine. You must trust me, because I trust you; that is why I was prepared to part ways with fifteen thousand rands of my precious money to get you out on bail, before they could coerce you, suck a confession out of you, and bring you into condemnation.

In anticipation of you agreeing to my proposal, I took the liberty of adding a DVD with notes. The DVD contains the best performances of female lawyers, both real and some Hollywood ones. You must watch the DVD and learn to emulate how they present themselves and their mannerisms; how they talk, walk and behave in court. Learn their tactics and how they interrogate witnesses and squeeze the truth out of them to their own advantage.

At the first day of your trial, you must tell the judge that you would like to represent yourself, and play ignorant. We must get them off guard. They will be expecting a kitty cat, but they will get a tigress!

I know communication won't be a problem, I've got your school records. Even though, you have not finished your degree, you were the best in your class.

So don't let fear send you to jail, speak like you mean it; confidently and articulately. Your freedom depends on how well you communicate during your trial.

Remember that they will be keeping tabs on you until the trial is over.

They are already following you, taking pictures and videos of you; so for the sake of your freedom, be on your best behaviour until your trial is over.

Legally yours,
The Associate

P.S. In case you're wondering how to get hold of me, don't worry, I will be a step behind you until your trial is over. All the best!"

After reading the note, she put her hands inside the envelope to see if the DVD was there, and she found it. But she didn't take it out of the envelope for fear that someone could be watching her.

While thinking about what she had just read and what she should do, a great fear seized her. She was terrified about the possibility of going to jail, losing her job, and ending up with a criminal record. She sat there in distress, her hands over her eyes. The bus stopped at her stop, but she didn't get off. After waiting for a while and other passengers starting to complain, the bus driver, Mpho, looked in his rear view mirror. When he saw her, he called, "Bonelwa, are you getting off, or are you going somewhere else?"

The calling out of her name woke her out of the sorrowful slumber.

"Yes, yes, thank you, Mpho!"

"No problem. See you tomorrow."

"Okay, thanks."

On the way to her small apartment, she kept on looking back to see if she was being followed, but she saw no one following her.

When she arrived home, she locked the door behind her and pushed the couch against the door.

"What have I done? I should've stayed in Cape Town and finished my studies. Now I have ruined my life, and for what? For a guy who doesn't even give a damn about me!" the voice of regret tormented her.

She went to her room, locked the door and pushed the dresser against it, and lay on her bed and cried for fear and regret. She fell asleep in her clothes.

Her sleep was disturbed by an early morning call from her manager, asking her to come to the bank as soon as she could.

On the day of her arrest, the bank management had an after-hours meeting to deliberate on her case. After reaching a decision, they called the head office with their decision. The head office dispatched Mr. Mokwena, the bank's Public Relations Officer, to spin the media attention the bank was getting from the case into a positive marketing campaign.

The Public Relations Officer arrived at the bank early in the morning, and that is why Bonelwa was called to come to the bank. When she arrived at the bank, she found the bank surrounded by reporters and TV crews. She wanted to turn back when she saw them, but it was too late because some of the reporters had already seen her and rushed her way to get some comments from her concerning the case. She was escorted by the bank's security until she entered the bank and immediately taken to the boardroom, where Mokwena was waiting for her with his team.

After they had been formally introduced, she told them the whole story, but spared them some details that were not relevant to the court case.

Mokwena and his team asked a few questions and when they were satisfied, she was released to go home on paid leave until the trial was over. Then, depending on the verdict, she may or may not return to work, since the bank could not employ people with criminal records.

When he was ready to address the media, Mokwena asked the security team to escort Bonelwa to her transport, while he called the media for a brief press conference. He went out and called the media aside to be addressed, and as the media complied, Bonelwa was escorted out of the bank and led to her transport.

With all set, and the media quiet and attentive to be briefed, Mokwena began his address by saying:

"Firstly, I want to say, that the bank stands by Ms. Hlazo.

Secondly, we believe she is innocent, until we are proven otherwise by a court of law.

Thirdly, the bank offered Ms. Hlazo, legal support. However, she politely declined the bank's help, citing that she didn't want to drag the bank into her personal battle, and we have respected her decision.

So, it is going to be a twenty-two year old girl, against one of the biggest and most influential law firms in Gauteng. Like the Bible's David and Goliath, may the God who helped David, help this young girl against the mighty giants against her."

"Amen!" was the lonely reply of a Christian reporter.

He was immediately scourged by the looks of his colleagues.

After the tension had subsided, Mokwena took centre stage again saying, "I will now be taking some questions from you."

The reporters responded by raising their hands, and waiting to be picked by Mokwena to ask him questions.

"Let us start with you, the one who shouted 'Amen!'"

"Thank you, Sir, I appreciate the opportunity. My questions are: Has Ms. Hlazo been disciplined this morning? Has she been fired? Or is her job on the line?"

"Let's start with your second and last question. No, she has not been fired, but I must be frank with you; the bank does not employ any person with a criminal record. Her job is not in jeopardy, unless of course she is found guilty by a court of law. In that case, the bank would be left with no choice but to act according to its policy, which in the case of a guilty verdict, Ms. Hlazo would be immediately dismissed. And to answer your first question—no, she has not been disciplined this morning. We just needed to brief her on the decisions that the bank has made regarding her case, and we also wanted to be updated by her, that's all."

"Thank you, Sir"

"Next... You there."

"Thank you, Sir. Do you think this incident will affect the image and reputation of the bank?"

"I sincerely doubt that. Our customers are people that believe in, and strive to uphold, the constitution which guarantees all citizens innocence until proven guilty. So, I believe they will stand with us in our decision to support Ms. Hlazo until she is proven guilty of the charges laid against her, and only then, can we re-evaluate our stance. Besides, it is a well-known fact that the bank is deeply involved in and supports leading organizations that are in the forefront fighting against the abuse of women and children. The bank donates large sums of money to such organizations so that together we can stop the violation of the basic human rights of women and children."

And so, with each question posed by the reporters, Mokwena used it as an opportunity, to paint a picture-perfect image of his bank, and made his bank appear as the champion of the poor and marginalized.

CHAPTER TWELVE

B y the time she arrived home, Bonelwa found a new sealed envelope in her mailbox. She quickly opened it and found a new note from The Associate, and a phone inside. She went into her apartment and sat down to read the note.

"Dear Ms. Hlazo, I presume you have taken my advice. I am afraid we have a big problem. As I suspected, I have confirmed that the judge is with them. I don't know yet, if Mafoko has paid him or is blackmailing him.

So, our best shot at getting you a fair trial, is to pray that the presiding judge invites two impartial assessors to help with the factual findings; and hope that at least one of them is unlikely to be bribed— which they will probably try to do. Mafoko is a conniving snake, he will not take any chances; he will use any method, however devious, to win this case.

That is why his own son, Tau, doesn't want to work with him— because he knows his Dad's ways are devious and he doesn't like it.

The mobile with this note sends encrypted messages that cannot be hacked. I'm the only one that has the number. Please don't use it for anything else but receiving and sending texts in communication with me.

The selection of the two assessors will begin just before the trial begins. Let's just hope one of them is a woman, which will more likely sympathize with your defence.

You must always remember, though they have the cops that arrested you, the judge and your court appointed lawyer, they still have to abide by the rules during the trial.

So, don't be afraid; focus and learn to act, talk and think like a lawyer, and fight for your freedom.

I will keep in touch.

Legally Yours,

The Associate"

Determined to fight for her freedom, Bonelwa put the DVD on and found a pen and a notebook to take notes.

She watched the DVD from the beginning to the end and took some notes.

Out of all the lawyers on the DVD, she picked one and focused all her energy on emulating her garb, mannerisms, speech and tactics, until she had mastered it all.

Once the assessors were selected, it was time for the trial to begin.

Tau's father was being represented by the top lawyer of his firm, who learned from Mafoko how to win at any cost, and like Mafoko, had never lost a single case.

On the first day of the trial, as instructed by The Associate, she played a clueless twenty-two-year-old black girl; she dismissed her court appointed lawyer and requested the judge to allow her to defend herself. The judge granted her request and the trial began.

The leading prosecuting attorney eloquently made his opening statement and painted a gruesome portrait of Bonelwa, promising the presiding judge and two assessors that after all the evidence had been presented, the court would come to the same conclusion. The presiding judge and two assessors glanced at Bonelwa sitting there, but couldn't bring themselves to agree in their minds with the prosecution. When the prosecution rested, it was Bonelwa's time to make her opening statement.

The judge asked her if she would like to make her opening statement, she said, "Yes," and started looking for it among her disorganized papers.

The judge's opinion of Bonelwa was poisoned by Mafoko. He was told she was a cold-hearted, manipulative murderer. But looking at her all alone at the defence desk, helpless and clueless, she reminded the judge of one of his daughters, and he felt pity for her; especially when he looked at the prosecution made up of the best lawyers in the country.

The corrupt judge's conscience would not allow him to destroy the young woman's life. He just could not go through with it. So, while they all waited for her to make her opening statement, the judge faked having a heart attack and was rushed to the hospital. At the hospital he asked for his doctor, who also was his friend. His doctor came and took over, and the judge told his doctor everything, asking him to book him off for two months, which the doctor did.

Meanwhile, back at the court, the case was adjourned until a replacement judge was found.

Two days later, the prosecution, the defendant, and the two assessors were notified that Judge Maria Maluleka would be taking over the case and that all parties involved should be in court on Monday to resume the trial.

On the very day that she received the notification from the court, Bonelwa, heard a strange beep while she was watching the DVD and taking notes. She paused the DVD, to hear where the strange beep was coming from, and that is when she noticed the last envelope she had received from The Associate moving on the top of the coffee table. She reached out for the envelope and took out the mobile and saw that she had received a text message from The Associate, which read:

"Hi, I have very good news for us! The new judge is an honest one. She cannot be bribed, she loves justice, and she is an impartial judge. She believes everyone deserves a fair trial in her courtroom, and she is intimidated by no one. Now that we have the right judge and assessors, get ready for Monday and let the tigress come out to devour your enemies.

I will see you there; be strong, you'll make it."

Encouraged, Bonelwa pressed play and continued her training.

Monday morning, she showed up at court dressed like a lawyer. She was wearing a black suit with a white shirt, high heels, and even carried a lawyer's briefcase. After all was set, the trial resumed.

She made an impressive opening statement, which left the prosecution flabbergasted.

The prosecution called its first witness, Detective Sizane, one of the arresting officers. The leading prosecuting attorney then questioned him.

"Detective Sizane, what was your observation when you arrested the defendant?"

"She seemed very worried and anxious, like someone who had something to hide. She had a guilty look on her face, but what surprised me the most was that she was not surprised to see us, as if somehow she knew that we would be coming to arrest her," Sizane replied.

"Thank you, Detective Sizane. I have no other questions, Your Honour."

It was Bonelwa's turn to question the witness, so she got up and confidently walked toward the witness stand, and looking straight into Detective Sizane's eyes, she posed her question:

"Detective Sizane, were you in possession of a warrant of arrest when you arrested me?"

"Objection, Your Honour!" the prosecution shouted.

"On what grounds, Counsellor?" the judge replied.

"The witness is a police officer, the defendant shouldn't subject the witness to questions that undermine his integrity."

"Objection overruled, the witness must answer the question," the judge ruled.

"Detective Sizane, I would like to remind you that lying under oath is a crime, so please answer the question truthfully. Were you in possession of a warrant of arrest, when you arrested me?"

"No. we didn't…"

"Please answer with a yes or no. Did you have a warrant for my arrest?"

"No."

"No further questions, Your Honour."

The prosecution looked at her in disbelief, as she walked confidently back to her seat.

Tau's dad was angry at her; his shady plan to dump her in prison was not going according to plan. But, Tau looked at her with great admiration.

Wounded, and baying for revenge, the prosecution called their second witness, Detective Makgatho, the other arresting officer.

The leading prosecuting lawyer stood in front of the witness, his mind ran to and fro, seeking the best way to incriminate the defendant and make the charges against her stick. So, looking at the detective and turning his gaze on the two assessors, he posed his question:

"Detective Makgatho, could you please share with the court what you have found out about Ms. Hlazo during your investigation?"

"Yes, the first thing that really alarmed us was that Ms. Hlazo had been secretly stalking Mr. Tau Mafoko, the brother of the victim. After we received complaints that she had made threats against the life of Mr. Tshepo Mafoko, who is but one step away from death at this very moment, we…"

His testimony was interrupted by Mr. Mafoko's fake tears. Mr. Mafoko cried and sobbed as a mother who lost her only child and the court's attention turned to the mourning father.

"I am so sorry… my son could die any moment now!" He burst into greater tears and succeeded in touching one of the assessors.

The leading attorney, who was analysing the assessors' reaction while his boss was pouring fake tears, gave his boss the signal that it was enough and the fake tears stopped.

"Detective Makgatho, please proceed with your testimony."

"I know this is a difficult time for the family, I'll try to be more cautious as I proceed. We found that Ms. Hlazo is a manipulative, seductive young woman with a vendetta against all men. She seduces and sleeps with her victims and makes them fall in love with her. When that is accomplished, she then dumps that person for the mere pleasure of inflicting pain on his heart, in order to avenge herself from a heartbreak she had previously endured.

Because a man broke her heart, she decided that all men must pay. She was supposed to be finishing her degree in Journalism in Cape Town next year, but revenge has brought her to Gauteng. Her parents don't even know that she is here! I think she needs to see a psychiatrist—she needs help!"

Bonelwa was caught off guard; her personal life was exposed for everyone to see. She felt her privacy was invaded, and as all eyes in the courtroom turned their gaze to her, she felt tried, judged and condemned. She wanted to pack her belongings and run. While the courtroom was still tense with silence, and before she could recover from the mighty blow given to her character, which consequently cast a dark shadow on her credibility, the leading prosecutor put the nails in her coffin with the stinging words, "No further questions, Your Honour." He gave the defendant a look of disgust and shook his head before taking a seat.

All Bonelwa could hear in her mind after he had said those stinging words was, "You are a poor little sick lady. You are insane and guilty. Get help, Slut. You're going to a prison for crazy people."

She didn't know how to recover from that and became distracted. She had no one to consult with; and no one to help her to recover.

After waiting for a while, the judge cleared her throat to wake her up from wonderland, but she didn't awaken. So the judge raised her voice, and with an admonishing tone she said, "Would the defence like to question the witness, or should we all take a break? I am tired myself, so let's take an hour break and we will resume after that."

She felt pity for the poor girl fighting for her freedom all alone against the pit bulls of the courtroom, who had just shown their true colours. They didn't play fair and were there to win, ready to use any dirty trick to secure victory, which put the judge on the defensive against them.

She saw the prosecution smiling and sharing their early victory.

"If they must win in my courtroom, they must win it fairly," the judge said to herself. She then rose and went to her private chamber.

Bonelwa left the courtroom humiliated, and contemplating running away. She rushed to the restroom, threw up, and cried. While she was still crying and wallowing in self-pity, she received a text message from The Associate saying,

"You must pull yourself together and fight back. Unless you want to go to jail and spend time with real crazy people. I've left new information under your notes. Use it to bring Detective Makgatho down from his high horse, and wipe away that prideful smile from the prosecution's face. Stop crying like a kitten, and start roaring like a tigress!"

"That's right, I am a tigress, not a kitten. They want to play dirty? I can do dirty! They've messed with the wrong girl!"

She washed her face, left the restroom walking tall and confidently, and went straight to the courtroom to study the new information The Associate had left for her.

A few moments later, the prosecution, the assessors and all attending the trial returned. Shortly after that, the judge also returned. They were all asked to rise, and then were seated after the judge was seated. The judge banged her gavel and the trial resumed. The witness was requested to return to the witness stand.

Then the judge looked at Bonelwa with a supportive look and asked, "Is the defence ready to question the witness?"

Bonelwa replied with an assertive, "Yes, Your Honour!"

She got up out of her seat and clapped her hands in sarcastic applause as she walked toward the witness.

"What an incredible performance! Very moving and touching, I must say, I am impressed! First the crocodile tears from the boss and then, a brilliant performance by the star witness—a caring detective. Perfect combination, but all a show to deceive!"

"Objection! Your Honour, the defendant is insinuating without providing any evidence for it!" the prosecution shouted.

"Sustained. Ms. Hlazo, please get to the point," the judge ruled.

"Yes, Your Honour. Detective Makgatho, were you officially on duty when you arrested me?"

"I don't know what you mean."

"Okay, let me rephrase the question for you. On the day of my arrest, were you on duty, or off duty at the time?"

"Objection, Your Honour!" the prosecution shouted.

"On what grounds, Counsellor?" the judge replied.

"The witness is a detective; the defendant shouldn't subject the witness to questions that undermine the sacrifices he has to make for his country."

"Objection overruled. The witness must answer the question," the judge ruled.

"Detective Makgatho, I would like to remind you that lying under oath is a crime, so please answer the question truthfully. Were you on duty, or off duty, when you arrested me with your partner?"

"Off duty," Makgatho mumbled, ashamed.

"Thank you for your honesty, Detective Makgatho. So, you were off duty when you entered the bank with your partner to arrest me without a warrant of arrest, is that correct?"

"My partner needed help and needed me to support him, so I had to cut my off day short, to serve my country."

"Detective Makgatho, please answer the question with a yes or no. Did you and your partner arrest me illegally while you were officially off duty?"

"Objection! Your Honour, the defendant is insinuating without providing any evidence for it!"

"Your Honour, I have evidence that proves that Detective Makgatho had no business to arrest me while off duty!"

"Objection overruled, the witness must answer the question," the judge ruled.

"Detective Makgatho, were you officially off duty when you arrested me?"

"Yes!" he replied, angry.

The judge frowned at him.

"Let me get this straight, are you saying that you arrested the defendant illegally, when you were not officially on duty?" the judge asked, annoyed.

"Yes, Your Honour."

"Is the defence done with questioning the witness?" The judge asked, disappointed at the prosecution.

"Not yet, Your Honour," Bonelwa replied.

"Please proceed, Ms. Hlazo," said the judge.

"Detective Makgatho, are you aware that you are under investigation by the NPA for tampering with evidence, withholding information, falsifying evidence, taking bribes, taking the law into your own hands, money laundering and other charges? Are you aware of these charges against you by the NPA?"

"Yes."

"Just one last question... When you were spending time with your son on that day, did you come off duty to act illegally by your desire to serve your country, or by your greedy heart that just couldn't pass on the generous offer that Mr. Mafoko made to any anyone who would help him take vengeance on me because I've broken up with his son?"

"Objection! Your Honour, the defendant is insinuating without providing any evidence for it!"

"Sustained. Ms. Hlazo, please refrain from any insinuations."

"I have no further questions, Your Honour."

She once again walked like a victor to her desk, leaving behind a detective with a shattered reputation, almost impossible to be restored, and the prosecution asking themselves who was helping her, as they left the court for the day.

CHAPTER THIRTEEN

O
n the second day of the trial, the prosecution returned to court with a vengeful spirit. They were not accustomed to losing court battles with their equals, let alone losing to a little girl representing herself.

So, they came ready to bury her alive.

After the judge had opened the session that day, the prosecution called Mrs. Zuki Mafoko as their witness. The pregnant woman was helped to the witness stand and made to promise by an oath to tell nothing but the truth.

"Mrs. Mafoko, were you in the room when the defendant made threats against the life of your brother-in-law?"

"Yes, I was."

"Would you mind telling the court what you heard the defendant saying against the life of the victim?"

"It was on our wedding day, everything was going well until I couldn't find my husband, and when I was told where he was, I went to get him. That is when I found him asking the defendant what she was doing there, and naturally, I was angry to see her at my wedding, especially after what she did to my younger brother…"

"Mrs. Mafoko, sorry to interrupt, but not everyone here is acquainted with what the defendant had done to your younger brother, could you please tell the court before you proceed with your testimony?" the leading persecutor intercepted.

"Okay… the defendant knew that my brother suffers from asthma and he gets short breath attacks when he finds himself in very stressful situations. Knowing that, she seduced him, made him fall madly in love with her, and plotted for my brother to find her in bed with one of her other boyfriends, just to hurt him and get back at me and my husband. My brother came to me that night and told me and my husband what had happened to him. He didn't want to be alone, which was truly an act of God, because if he had been alone that night, my brother would've died!" she said, bursting into tears.

To aggravate the witness' distress, the prosecution asked for a glass of water for the witness. After drinking the whole glass of water, she resumed her testimony by saying, "You can all imagine how angry I was to see the woman who attempted to murder my brother at my wedding! I wanted her out of my wedding party as soon as possible. So, while we were exchanging words, my husband suggested that we go to a private chamber and discuss things there. That is when I heard the defendant, with my own ears saying, 'I promise you Tau, I will dump Tshepo and hurt him so deeply, that it will make what his ex-wife did to him look like a picnic. I will hurt him so badly, that it will drive him really insane this time. Who knows what he will do this time, maybe commit suicide? I don't know, only time will tell.'

"Mrs. Mafoko, were those her exact words or are you paraphrasing what she said?"

"Those were her exact words."

"Are you saying to the court that the defendant, openly conspired against the life of the victim?

"Yes."

"What was your reaction after you heard her making threats against the life of the victim?"

"I was terrified because I knew she was not just making empty threats. After what she did to my brother, I've learned to take her threats very seriously!"

"Do you think the defendant is capable of murder?"

"Yes, I know she is more than capable!"

"No further questions, Your Honour."

Bonelwa got up, straightened her suit and shirt, approached the witness stand, and looked into Zuki's eyes for a good while, until Zuki blushed.

"Mrs. Mafoko, you and I used to be best of friends, is that correct?"

"Yes, that is correct."

"Would you mind telling the court, why we are no longer best friends?"

"I don't know, I guess we fell out of friendship, as many others have."

"You don't know? Okay, let me refresh your memory. We stopped being best friends because I found my boyfriend, who had intentions of proposing to me, half naked in your room! So, we are no longer friends because you stole my boyfriend, is that correct?"

"I guess so."

"Please answer the question with yes or no. Did you steal my boyfriend?"

"Yes, but…"

"No buts, Mrs. Mafoko, a yes will do."

"Let's talk about your wedding, where I made the threats that I am accused of. Were your wedding venue, theme colour, bride's dress and groom's suit, food and drinks your idea?"

"No."

"Whose idea were they?"

"Yours."

"So, you are admitting that you stole my boyfriend, as well as the ideas of my dream wedding, which I told you in confidence because we were best friends, and you made it your own dream. Is that correct?"

"Yes."

"How do you sleep at night, Zuki, with a stolen husband and a stolen dream? Or do you spend sleepless nights afraid that as you have stolen him away from me, someone else might snatch him and your fantasy of a marriage away from your fake life?"

Zuki gave her no answer.

"Your Honour, I have no further questions for a witness who clearly doesn't live her own life, but falsely lives other people's lives!"

She turned her back on the witness and went to take her seat, swaggering, and leaving the presiding judge and two assessors questioning Zuki's character. Zuki looked at her frenemy walking away, with evil indignation, while the prosecution looked at her almost with admiration, as a worthy opponent.

Because it was close to lunch break, the judge requested that they resume after lunch. Both parties agreed.

Lunch ended and the court proceedings were resumed. Without any further delays, the prosecution called Mr. Tau Mafoko as their next witness.

"Mr. Mafoko, I believe you and the defendant share a personal history, you dated while you were in university, is that correct?"

"Yes, that is correct."

"What happened, why did you break up?"

"I fell in love with someone else."

"You mean, your lovely wife?"

"Yes."

"What was the defendant's reaction after learning that you fell in love with someone else?"

"She didn't take it very well, and I expected that, but the thing I didn't expect was that she would turn so violent and vindictive—to the point that we should constantly watch our backs for the rest of our lives!"

"Could you show the court what she did to your arm and how she did it?"

Tau took off his jacket and rolled back his shirt, showing the dark spots on his right arm, and said, "The night the defendant found out that I was in love with her best friend at the time, I was in my wife's room. The defendant came in and when she found out that I was there, she started hitting me with her high heels. I tried to protect my face with my right arm and asked her to stop, but she didn't; she only stopped when she noticed that her high heel was dripping with my blood. She stopped hitting and approached my wife, pointed her left index finger at her and said, 'You, Ms. Little Slut, are deserving of death right now!'"

"Were those her exact words?"

"Yes, word for word."

"Do you think she meant it?"

"At the time, I thought she was just angry, but after all that has happened, I think she meant every word she said! We're constantly living in fear, especially with my wife pregnant."

"Why do you say that?"

"Because she keeps on following us, we left Cape Town hoping to start afresh, but she dropped out of university and got herself a job next to where I work. She stalks me and my wife any chance she gets. What if one day she finds my pregnant wife all alone? I don't even want to think about that, it horrifies me. With the hatred she's caring inside her for me and my wife, anything is possible!"

"Are you saying your wife's life and yours is in danger?"

"Yes, that is what I am saying. Unless something is done by the authorities, anything can happen to me, my wife and our unborn child."

"That is a very serious thing, Mr. Mafoko, have you reported it to the police?"

"My wife suggested we get a restraining order against her, but I was afraid that could enrage her even further and prompt her to do something harmful to us."

"What would make you and your wife feel safe, Mr. Mafoko?"

"I think the break up has affected her, mentally; she must be confined in a rehabilitation centre until she has recovered. Only then can we feel safe. Until then, we'll live in fear and terror."

"No further questions, Your Honour."

After the leading prosecuting attorney has taken his seat, Bonelwa rose and clapped all the way to the witness stand, saying, "Ladies and gentlemen, please give a round of applause for the star of our show, Mr. Tau Mafoko, for an outstanding performance of inconveniently leaving incriminating details out of his testimony! Mr. Mafoko, you deserve an award for the best selective memory I've ever seen!"

Then looking at Tau, she asked, "Mr. Mafoko, were you my first boyfriend?"

"I don't know what you mean by that."

"Did you take away my virginity?"

"Yes."

"When you wanted to have sex with me the first time, I said to you that I couldn't do it because I had a family tradition to keep, is that correct?"

"Yes, that is correct."

"But you didn't respect my wishes, why is that?"

"I thought you didn't really mean it, and that you were just play-ing hard to get."

"I see. Mr. Mafoko… are you a trustworthy person? I mean, do you keep your promises? And can we trust what comes out of your month?"

"Yes, I am."

"Would you mind telling the court, why, after resisting your sex-ual advances, I finally offered you my virginity?"

"I guess you were ready at the time."

"Mr. Mafoko, are you mocking this court of law? Is this a big gag for you?"

"No, not at all."

"Mr. Mafoko, you may be a good lawyer, but you are a very ter-rible liar, and disastrous comedian! Therefore, I would like to kindly remind you not to omit any information while under oath, for you know the law better than I do. Can we proceed and take things seri-ously?"

"Yes, please do."

"Mr. Mafoko, what did you promise me in exchange for my virginity?"

"I promised to marry you."

"Have you kept that solemn, lifetime promise you made to me?"

"No, I haven't."

"Does that give me the right to call you a liar and untrustworthy?"

Tau bowed his head in shame as he pondered how to answer truthfully and satisfactorily, without injuring his credibility.

"While you are thinking about the answer to that question, let us talk about the incident that took place in your so-called wife's room at the University of Cape Town, when I brutally marred your delicate arm with my high heel. Where were you when I hit your arm?"

"I was in Zuki's room."

"Tau, you are an intelligent man, please do not degrade the dignity of this courtroom. I already stated affirmatively that the incident took place in your wife's room, therefore, you had to be in the room when that happened. Is that clear enough for you, or should I put my question into a much lower grade of English for you to understand me correctly?"

"I get it."

"Thank you, Mr. Mafoko. Now let me rephrase the question for you, where were you inside Zuki's room?"

"Under the bed."

"See, Mr. Mafoko, it is not that hard to tell the truth. Now, I understand that would be a shameful position for a grown man to find himself in, unless he was doing evil and had to suddenly hide. So why were you hiding under the bed?"

"I didn't want you to see me there. I didn't want to hurt your feelings."

"That was very sweet and thoughtful of you. But if that was true, and you were really sincere about not wanting to hurt my feelings, you would not have slept with my so-called best friend, don't you agree?"

"I suppose so."

"So, you were hiding because you were cheating on me with my best friend, and when you realized that it was me at the door, your guilty conscience prompted you to hide like criminals do when they see an agent of the law! Can I call you a cheater?"

"I guess so... but I have changed."

"Mr. Mafoko, cheaters don't change; besides, it is your so-called wife that you have to convince, not me or this court."

Then turning to the presiding judge and the two assessors, she posed her final questions with prose.

"Mr. Mafoko, by your own admission, you are a manipulative liar, a shameless cheater and an untrustworthy person. Isn't it ironic that a person with such a foul character as yourself should try to advise this truthful court of law? Would you believe a manipulative liar, a shameless cheater and an untrustworthy person?"

"No."

"No further questions, Your Honour."

After saying those stinging words, she once again walked to her desk as a ramp model, leaving behind a flabbergasted Tau and the prosecution stung by her charm and courage.

As the trial progressed, more witnesses were called, mostly by the prosecution who were desperate to win. When they saw that they didn't stand a chance to send her to prison, as their original plan was, they pressed hard to convince the presiding judge and the two assessors that she was insane, unstable, and should be sent to a mental institution.

When all their witnesses had testified, they called Bonelwa to the witness stand to be questioned by the prosecution, and she complied.

While she sat on the witness stand, she prepared herself to answer the trick and hard questions the prosecution would ask her.

"Your Honour, the prosecution would like to present new evidence that is crucial to its case. Your Honour, I kindly request that Exhibit A be admitted as evidence and shown to the court," the leading prosecuting attorney said confidently, as he approached the judge.

"Counsellors, please approach the bench," the judge requested.

The leading prosecuting attorney approached the bench. The judge looked at Bonelwa and said, "You too, Ms. Hlazo, you have to step off the witness stand and be your counsellor for this."

Bonelwa quickly stepped off the witness stand and approached the bench.

"Did you know about this new evidence, Ms. Hlazo?"

"No, Your Honour, I did not—until now."

"Counsellor, why was this evidence not presented before, along with other evidence?"

"Your Honour, the prosecution was not in possession of the new evidence, until this morning."

"What is it, Counsellor?" the judge asked.

"Your Honour, it is a video that shows the defendant making threats against the life of the victim."

"Ms. Hlazo, because you are not an attorney and might not be familiar with the law concerning this, it is my duty to inform you of all your rights. You have the right to contest the new evidence, so that it may not be admitted and presented to the court. Do you understand, Ms. Hlazo?"

"Yes, Your Honour, I understand, and thank you. However, I don't want to contest the new evidence. If you permit it, the counsellor can present it to the court."

"Are you certain about this, Ms. Hlazo?"

"Yes, Your Honour."

"Alright, you may return to your places, and the prosecution may proceed in presenting the new evidence to the court," the judge ruled.

The new evidence was then handed to the court's assistant and the video was played to the court. The video showed Bonelwa threatening Tau to hurt Tshepo so badly that it would lead him to commit suicide.

After the video was played, the prosecution turned its gaze on Bonelwa and said,

"Ms. Hlazo, is that you making threats against the life of Mr. Tshepo Mafoko, in the video that was just played?"

"Yes, that is me."

"Why, Ms. Hlazo? Why would you make such threats against the life of an innocent person?"

"Because I was angry with his brother."

"Why were you angry with his brother? Because he left you and married someone else?"

"Yes, because he deceived me into giving him my virginity without having any intentions of marrying me, he took me for a fool!"

"Is your pain worth the death of an innocent person?"

"Have you been hurt, Counsellor? I mean, has your wife ever cheated on you with your boss or best friend?"

"Ms. Hlazo, I will do the questioning, please answer the question."

"No, my pain is not worth the death of an innocent person; however, in a war, there is always collateral damage."

"Ms. Hlazo, are you aware that Mr. Tshepo Mafoko may die at any moment because of your reckless, revengeful behaviour? Someone's son, someone's brother is on the verge of death, Ms. Hlazo. Do you even care? Do you have a heart? Are you aware of the pain you have caused to this family? Tshepo's mother cries incessantly at his bedside, knowing that the only thing keeping her son alive is a machine! And it is all your fault, Ms. Hlazo; the blood of Tshepo Mafoko is in your hands!" the prosecutor said, dramatizing and playing to the emotions of the court.

He propagated the two assessors with his questions that he wanted no answers for, and even the judge gave Bonelwa a strange look for the first time. But none was more crushed by the forceful questioning than Bonelwa. She burst into tears of regret on the witness stand.

The leading prosecutor looked at crying Bonelwa, and felt pity. She reminded him of his own daughter. He looked at his boss for direction, his heartless boss gave him the signal to push her to the breaking point. His heart disagreed with his boss, but his mind had a job to do. So he proceeded.

"Ms. Hlazo, crying is not going to help Tshepo Mafoko back from the verge of death! A confession and an apology to his grieving family, would be of far greater value and perhaps help the family to cope with this painful situation! Every second that passes, the Mafoko family has to force their hearts to prepare for the ultimate pain of separation—the untimely death of their loved one, and all this pain is caused by your sinister games of revenge!"

Seeing that Bonelwa was disoriented and vulnerable due to the serious accusations against her; he pressed hard for an incriminating confession from her.

"Ms. Hlazo, did you intentionally put Tshepo Mafoko in a coma, kept alive only by a life support machine?"

"I... I... I don't know what you mean," she mumbled.

"Okay... Let me ask you another question before I rephrase the question. Were you aware that Tshepo Mafoko had a mental breakdown and had just recently recovered, though he was still very much vulnerable?"

"Yes, I was aware."

"Knowing that, you still pushed him off the edge of sanity, put the gun of suicide in his hand, and shouted at him to pull the trigger, didn't you?"

"No, I didn't ask him to commit suicide!" she shouted in her own defence.

"Ms. Hlazo, throughout this trial, you have constantly warned the witnesses that they are under oath. Therefore, I would like to remind you that perjury is a serious offense. The general perjury statute under the law of this country, classifies perjury as a serious crime and you could be sentenced to prison for up to five years, for lying in court. Hence, I plead that you answer the following question truthfully.

"Did you wilfully hurt Tshepo Mafoko in a way that would break him and drive him into the hands of death, just to get back at his brother?"

Bonelwa wiped her tears trying to face the grievous accusations laid against her, and deeply sought for an effective way to answer truthfully, without incriminating herself.

The question brought a loud and tense silence. The court waited with great anticipation for the answer that brought the case to trial. Yet, there was no answer from Bonelwa.

"Ms. Hlazo, please answer the question," the judge said.

"Could you please repeat the question?" Bonelwa asked the prosecutor.

"Did you wilfully hurt Tshepo Mafoko in a way that would break him and drive him into the hands of death, just to get back at his brother?" he asked again.

After a brief, thoughtful silence she replied, "Yes, I did, but…"

"No buts, Ms. Hlazo," the prosecution intercepted.

"Your Honour, I have no further questions."

As the prosecutor walked back to his seat and joined his celebrating team, all eyes in court were at Bonelwa; some had already passed a guilty verdict on her.

Seeing Bonelwa walk back to her desk with her head down and sitting nervously all by herself, the judge announced that the court would recess until the following day. She wanted to make sure that Bonelwa got a fair trial.

The next day, the prosecution entered the court with great pomp and sense of entitlement to victory.

Bonelwa on the other hand, entered the court nervous, still trying to recover from the grilling on the previous day.

The judge opened the session and indicated to both parties which instructions she intended to give the two assessors; and then asked the prosecution to present its closing argument.

The leading prosecutor confidently stepped forward to address the presiding judge and the two assessors.

"Ladies and Gentlemen, Ms. Hlazo is a young and seemingly harmless woman, who shed a few tears of regret on the witness stand, which might've caused some of you to feel sorry for her, which is perfectly normal. To be honest with you, I felt pity for her when I saw her crying too.

"However, the law is not based on feelings, but on principles that guide and protect the rights of every citizen of our nation. When someone violates the rights of others, they break the law and must be held accountable for it in a court of law, regardless of how we feel about them.

"Let us not forget that based on the evidence presented before you, Ms. Hlazo has plotted against the life of Tshepo Mafoko. She may cry a few tears in the courtroom, but by the time we leave this court, she will go back home and relish the right and freedom to enjoy the good things of this life; a right that she has forceful snatched away from Tshepo Mafoko! She will eat, drink, watch TV, among other things, but Tshepo Mafoko cannot do that, because Ms. Hlazo willingly pushed him into a state of unconsciousness, only an inch away from death…"

He continued to paint Bonelwa as an unstable young woman that need to be rehabilitated. After presenting most of his closing argument, he ended by saying, "The law requires that I prove, beyond reasonable doubt, that the defendant has conspired against the life of the victim and that she did it intentionally. I am glad that has been proved, not by me or by this court, but by the defendant herself!

"We have all heard with our ears the defendant confessing with her own mouth that she had wilfully conspired against the life of the victim.

"I am not here to prove that the defendant is a bad person or why she did it.

"All I am asking is that you hold her accountable for what she did, which is conspiring against the life of an innocent person, who at any time might leave this world, never to return again! Thank you."

The prosecution's closing arguments left the presiding judge and the two assessors with a serious look on their faces.

It was now time for the defence to make its closing arguments.

Bonelwa walked forward to face the presiding judge and the two assessors and she looked at each one, studying them, and then began her closing argument by saying, "Thank you, Ladies and Gentlemen, for your undivided attention in this very significant case.

"You have heard the prosecution trying to pin the attempted murder charges on me, but when they realized that they didn't have evidence to back up their bogus charges, they changed their tune and tried to convince you that I am an insane, unstable, and a revengeful young woman. Then, because they didn't have enough evidence to support their charges, they resorted to a personal attack and dirty tricks.

"My privacy has been invaded and my personal affairs made public to humiliate me. They have succeeded in belittling and humiliating me to a point I felt so sick in my stomach that I had to literally throw up! However, the prosecution failed to prove beyond a reasonable doubt that I have forced Tshepo Mafoko to attempt suicide.

"The evidence presented in this case has done nothing but to prove that I am a victim of betrayal and deception.

"I have been portrayed as an angry and bitter ex-girlfriend.

"Am I angry with Tau and Zuki Mafoko? You bet I am. I am enraged at them! I'm angry with Tau Mafoko for deceiving me, breaking my heart into pieces and stepping on each of the broken pieces; angry with Zuki Mafoko for betraying and stabbing me in the back and making a fool out of me!

"So, yes, I am very much angry with them. I want them to pay, and learn not to betray and hurt others.

"Unfortunately, the law makes no provision for the broken heart. Otherwise I would have taken them to court and demanded that Tau restores my virginity and Zuki restore the wholeness of my heart.

"Now, because the law doesn't provide for the matters of the heart, this is a case that must be settled out of court!

"My heart is broken. Will it ever heal? Honestly, I don't know. My virginity was taken away from me by deception. Will I ever get it back? Never in this life! Why didn't I run to court and open a case against Tau for breaking up with me and making me do things I never thought I would do? Because the law acknowledges that we were all created with free will, and the law has no power to force anyone to love someone; that is why all those wise men who wrote the constitution and the law, and God Himself, left man to make his own choice on whom to love. Therefore, I cannot sue Tau Mafoko for no longer loving me and loving someone else.

"Now my question to you, ladies and gentlemen of this court, is how then, when I stopped loving Tshepo Mafoko and broke my relationship with him (however wild my reasons may be), am I brought to court to answer why I have broken up with him? Don't I have the right to exercise my free will and choose whom to love, or is that reserved for special people only?

"Your Honour, I submit to you that I am only here because Tshepo Mafoko is the son of a very rich and powerful lawyer.

"Should the law be bent to accommodate Mr. Mafoko's ego and god-like complex, simply because he is rich and influential?

"Should I be sent to jail, or a mental institution, because I have broken up with a rich boy, who could not handle the pain like the rest of us, the children of the poor of this country, have to do daily? We nurse our pain, mend our hearts and try to move on, in spite of all our pain, sorrow and low self-esteem that comes with being rejected and cheated on. You don't see most of us jumping into a road with speeding cars, attempting suicide, do you?

"Shall I then be held accountable for someone attempting to commit suicide, simply because I broke up with him?

"Your Honour, you have in this case the opportunity to prove once and for all that our judicial system is impartial. It protects the rich and poor alike; it does not discriminate against the common people. Your decision today could become a milestone in our justice system. It is within your power to send a clear message that our judicial system is not, and will not, be intimidated or look favourably on those who have money, power and influence! Rather, it will treat every citizen of this country with respect, fairness and dignity, as envisioned by the founders of this great nation!

"Your Honour, it is your responsibility as a citizen of this country and the presiding judge in this trial, to uphold, defend and enforce these principles that our forefathers fought with all their might to guarantee us—the freedom and rights that we are privileged to enjoy.

"I am young, and have made many mistakes, and will probably make many more as I learn to navigate the world of adults.

"Here I am, my life and future is in your hands, handle it with care!"

She turned around and humbly walked to her desk to await her fate.

The judge looked at the young woman seated all by herself, taking on one of the biggest law firms in Gauteng, alone.

She admired her fearlessness, fierceness and self-determination to put up a fight to the very end. But what left the judge, and some members of the court, in awe was her gift to communicate and articulate her defence as a professional attorney.

The judge turned her attention to the two assessors and read instruction to them saying, "Assessors of this trial, when I tell you that a party must prove something, I mean that the party must persuade you by the evidence presented in court; what he or she is trying to prove is more likely to be true than not true. This is sometimes referred to as 'the burden of proof.'"

She continued by reading them some articles and explained some of the unfamiliar terms that the court heard and the relevant laws that should guide its deliberations. Then she advised the assessors to deliberate on the case, based on the evidence presented in court only.

After releasing the assessors, the judge announced that the court would recess until the assessors had finalized its deliberations.

After three days of intense deliberations, the assessors finally reached a unanimous consensus. A day later the court reconvened.

After opening the session, the judge was ready to sentence Bonelwa.

"Will the defendant please rise?" the judge intoned.

Then looking at Bonelwa, she said,

"On the count of harassment, I find the defendant guilty. On the count of stalking the plaintiffs, I find the defendant guilty. On the count of conspiring against the life of the victim, I find the defendant not guilty."

While Bonelwa was still standing and waiting for the judge to sentence her, the judge looked at her and pronounced the sentencing, "Ms. Hlazo, you are free to go!"

Bonelwa thanked the judge, relieved of all her fears.

"But before you go," said the judge, "I have a few words of advice for you. Please move on with your life. You are a bright and beautiful young woman. You have a great future ahead of you, don't throw it all away by wasting your energy pursuing a jerk that is not worthy of your love or time. Let go of your pain, focus on your studies and career, and let love find you—don't chase it. Young woman, your country needs your great talent. Who knows what you could become, if you just focus on your own life and move on! Did you hear me, Ms. Hlazo?"

"Yes, Your Honour, I heard you. Thank you."

Then the judge thanked the members of the court for their time and service, and banged the gavel saying, "This court is adjourned."

The prosecution left the courtroom with their heads down. They were greeted by the local media, eagerly waiting to get their questions answered but the only answer they got from the prosecution team was, "No comment!" as they rushed to get into their cars. No one was more ashamed than the powerful Mr. Mafoko, whose team was beaten by a little girl without any formal training in law.

Bonelwa sat outside the courtroom, trying to digest what had transpired.

"I almost went to jail or some psychiatric hospital!" she thought to herself.

After settling her troubled soul, she decided to go home. She was immediately greeted by the media waiting for her; reporters encircled her as each one of them sought to get his question answered. They all asked questions at once, leaving her perplexed and unable to answer any of their questions.

She lifted her right hand to get their attention and said, "Please, one question at time."

Once she got them all quieted down, she pointed at a female reporter to put her question forward.

"Thank you, Ms. Hlazo," the female reporter said. "How does it feel to beat the best lawyers in Gauteng, while defending yourself in court?" the reporter asked.

"I don't take it for granted, they are excellent lawyers and I respect them very much! The only reason I won the case, is that the truth was on my side. It doesn't matter how eloquent or good you are, or how much money or power you have, you can't beat the truth; the truth will always emerge victoriously, even if it is oppressed for a while. But to answer your question, it feels great to be acquitted by a court of law and win the case against the best lawyers in Gauteng!"

"Now that you have won the case, are you going to leave Tau and Zuki Mafoko alone?" asked another reporter.

"No, they've lost the right to be left alone when they betrayed me."

"Do you have any regrets for breaking up with Tshepo Mafoko, now that he has attempted to commit suicide because of your break up?" asked the reporter next to her, on her right side.

"No, but I pray that he recovers soon."

"Will you…" "Do you…" "What about…" some of the other reporters tried to put their question forward, but they were all intercepted by Bonelwa saying, "That is all for now, I need to get home and rest. It has been a long and tiring trial, thank you all!"

After saying that, she pushed her way past them and went to her apartment.

CHAPTER FOURTEEN

That day, when she arrived home, she took a dive into her bed with her clothes on and fell asleep. Her rest was interrupted by the strange beeping sound notifying her that she had received a new message from The Associate. She reached for her handbag to get the phone and read the text message.

"Congratulations, Ms. Hlazo! I hope you are enjoying your sweet victory over your enemies. But, I would like to congratulate you in person. Can we meet tomorrow at lunch time, at the restaurant opposite the bank?"

After thinking for a while, she replied.

"Yes, we can meet at one o'clock in the afternoon tomorrow."

"Okay, I will see you tomorrow. Enjoy the rest of your day," The Associate replied.

The next day, Bonelwa arrived at the restaurant earlier than the appointed time, booked a table and waited for The Associate to show up.

While she sipped on cocktail juice, her eyes fixed on reading the last chapter of her all-time favourite book for the fifth time, a voice pulled her back from the imaginary world to the real world.

"Hello Ms. Hlazo, we have not met before, but you can call me The Associate."

She took her eyes off the addictive pages, and holding her breath, she turned to see who The Associate was. Her eyes ran from his feet to his head, but it didn't take long to reach his head. For he was a very short sixty-one year old man. He was bald, had a big belly, and wore big glasses. Not really what she had envisioned in her wild mind. But she jumped from her seat and hugged him, saying, "Thank you for rescuing me! You saved me from going to jail or a psychiatric hospital."

She squeezed him tighter and said, "Thank you!" And before she let him go, she kissed him on the cheeks.

The old man giggled like a little boy who got his first kiss from his crush.

They sat opposite each other, perused the menu, and made their orders.

"I can't thank you enough for what you have done for me, I really appreciate it. If you ever need anything, with which I can be of assistance, please just let me know and I will gladly do it," she said.

"Please don't worry about paying me back. I've gotten my reward with your victory. Seeing Mafoko walk out of the court with his head down in humiliation, defeated by a young girl, liberated me from all my years of self-pity and shame. See, twenty years ago, I stood opposite Mafoko in court, he played dirty, won the case, and made me look stupid and naïve. And I was, for I was expecting him to play fair, but he doesn't play fair. It is against his nature. That is why it is going to be very hard for him to swallow the bitter defeat we have inflicted on his god-like, never lose a case ego…

So thank you, you have restored my self-esteem and dignity. And that is why I am here to personally invite you to our official celebration party for the victory over our number one enemy!" he said.

"I would love to, you can count me in. When and where is the party, The Associate?" she asked.

"You can call me Victor from now on. The party is this Friday at our offices, four streets away from here," he replied, taking out his business card and the invite.

"You will need the invite to get in, so please don't forget to bring it along with you on Friday," he said.

"Okay, I won't," she replied.

She read the details on his business card.

"Hold on, you are Tau's boss?" she asked.

"Yes, Tau works for me but he is not at all like his father, as far as business is concerned," he replied.

"I'm sorry, but I don't think it's a good idea for me to come to the party. I know this is difficult for him and his family, and I don't want to rub it on his face," she said, looking away from him.

"I agree, and I wouldn't want that either, which is why Tau won't be at the party," he assured her.

"If that is the case, then I will be there," she responded with a less tense voice.

Just then, the waiter brought their orders. As they ate, Victor told Bonelwa that the party would start at seven in the evening. After they ate, Victor called the waiter to bring the bill, settled it, and left Bonelwa eating her dessert while she finished reading her book.

On Friday when she arrived at the party, the place was filled with Gauteng's top-notch lawyers and their trophy girlfriends. As the party progressed, one thing became clear to her, all the lawyers at the party had one thing in common— they all hated Mafoko. And they didn't make any effort to hide it, but gladly partook in the celebration of his hard fall and defeat. As the alcohol in their blood stream increased, those with trophy girlfriends felt compelled to boast about their last bedroom conquest while parading their beautiful young women. Victor joined them and paraded Bonelwa through the night. Bonelwa felt out of place most of the night, but she played along until she left the party.

As time went by, Bonelwa and Victor continued to meet whenever an occasion arose.

Meanwhile, a few months later, Tau and Zuki welcomed their first child—a baby boy. It was a time of rejoicing for the Mafokos; for a while the joy of the newborn made them forget the terrible defeat they suffered at the hands of Bonelwa.

As days passed, the baby took centre stage of the Mafokos' life. He became their object of worship and adoration, as if nothing else mattered. Tau frowned at all the attention that his son was getting. He wrestled with the joy of having a son, as well as feeling jealous of his son for making him invisible to his family and wife. And to make it worse, Zuki became emotionally detached from him, oblivious to his coming in and going out, which made him a stranger in his own house. After a long weekend with many visitors coming in and out of his house, Tau murmured to himself as he played the role of a butler to his wife and son. He was only called when something was needed, and when that was taken care of, they would forget about him again. Frowning, he would return again to his lonely corner.

The next working day, he left home with his countenance fallen, and with his eyes almost tearing up, he sulked all the way to work. When he arrived at work, he skipped all the chit-chat he usually had with his close co-workers and went straight to his office, where he freely wallowed in self-pity, his mind wondering afar with wild thoughts. His conversation with himself was interrupted by the ring tone of his office line. Not in the mood to entertain any client, or anyone for that matter, he let the phone ring until it stopped, and then he took the handset off the hook.

A few moments later, his closest co-worker came into his office and asked him what was wrong with his phone, and told him that the boss was trying to get hold of him. He quickly put the handset back on the hook, and just when he was about to take his hand off the handset, the phone rang. Unwillingly, he picked up—it was his boss asking him to come up to his office. He left his office and went by the restroom to wash his face, put on his fake happy face, and went to see what his boss wanted.

When he arrived at his boss's office, he found the old man very excited. Tau's eyes popped out when he entered his boss's office and saw three new shirts, two new suits, two new pairs of shoes, five ties and two bottles of top-notch cologne on his desk. He wondered what all of these were supposed to mean and what it had to do with him, but he was hesitant to ask. His boss looked at him and said, "Are you okay, Tau?"

"Yes Sir, I'm fine, thank you for asking… and how are you doing today?" Tau replied.

His boss showed him some awkward dance moves, while he sang, "Tonight is the night!" And replied, "That's how I am feeling today, Tau."

"Good for you, Sir," Tau retorted, envying his boss's good mood.

"See Tau, tonight I have my first date with the most beautiful woman, I have ever seen!" the old man said. "But there is just one problem, I want to wear and smell my best, but I don't know which one of these will make me look my utmost best," he said. "And that is why I have called you here, to help me choose. I know you have good taste and by the looks of it, women like it; so which one of these do you suggest I wear?" he asked.

Tau stood there, his thoughts running to and fro, and gave him no answer.

"Tau, don't look so surprised. I know what you're thinking, 'Why is an old married man so excited about a date with a young woman?' One day when you're old like me, you'll understand. See Tau, a young, good-looking, tall and well-built man with a great job like you, can get any girl he wants. But it is not so for people like me. When I was in high school people made fun of me, and in university, girls were ashamed to be seen with me. So I tied myself to the books, for I knew, unless I was very successful, no woman would look at me, let alone date me."

"But Sir, your wife is very beautiful and she doesn't seem like a materialistic woman."

"Yes Tau, my wife is a very beautiful, intelligent, down to earth, and hard-working woman; and that is the problem. Tau, she could have any man she wanted, yet she chose me, and that is what troubles my soul. She doesn't need my money and she doesn't want it, so why is she still with me after all these years?"

"Maybe because she loves you, Sir."

Tau's answer got Victor to think for a while. Then he shook his head in disagreement and said, "Oh Tau, don't be naïve. People like me are unlovable. I believe she is with me because she feels pity for me…and that is worse than rejection. I can take rejection. I grew up being rejected, so I am used to it, but I can't take people feeling sorry for me, which is why I keep looking for love outside of my wife."

"Sir, forgive me if I am out of line here, but are you saying that your lovely wife has been married to you for twenty-five years, twenty-five years in the prime of her life she devoted to you, and had four children with you, simply because she feels pity for you? Sorry Sir, I beg to differ."

Victor once again went quiet, deep in thought.

"Anyway, enough about my wife, it's ruining my mood for tonight."

While the words were still in his mouth, his office line rang. He picked up—it was his secretary letting him know that someone wanted to see him.

"She is here!" he said, grabbing some of the stuff from the desk to hide.

"Who is here?" Tau asked.

"My date for tonight. Tau please don't just stand there, help me hide the rest of the stuff, she will be here at any time," he whispered.

Victor took the ties and shoved them into the drawers, Tau took the two bottles of cologne and put them in his pocket, and the two turned their gaze to the glass window and saw her walking toward them. She was smoking hot in a red dress and black high heels with her hair let down.

"Wow!" Tau exclaimed, his mouth wide open.

"I told you! She makes me forget I am married and when I remember I am married, I don't want to be married. Do you get me?" Victor asked.

"Wow!" Tau replied, his eyes fixed on her.

Victor opened the door to let her in, Tau stood there, his eyes popped out and his mouth open.

"Hi Victor," she greeted.

"Hi Nelwa," Victor greeted back, his eyes all-over her body.

"I am sorry, I didn't know you had company," Bonelwa said.

"Hi Tau."

"Hi... Bonelwa, what a surprise," Tau replied.

"It's okay, he was just leaving," Victor said, raising his eyebrow and signalling Tau to leave his office.

"That won't be necessary, I won't be long. I have to go back to work. I just came to bring you a healthy lunch," Bonelwa said and handed Victor the lunch.

"Okay, thank you... it's very kind of you," Victor replied, words barely coming out of his mouth.

"I have to go now," she said and left.

The men watched her going until she turned.

"Wow! That was something..." Tau said.

"Yes, she makes me feel alive and young, and the best part is that she is very intelligent. We can talk for hours without talking about stupid TV shows or celebrities or any other vain thing. She can hold a conversation to the point I can feel mentally connected to her. And she doesn't want me to buy her any expensive gifts; I've offered many times, but she has turned me down. She has never once asked for money or made me pay for anything. Last week she insisted she pay the bill. What a lovely young woman; if I was not married, I would ask her to marry me right away..." Victor said and continued to tell Tau the very things that attracted him to Bonelwa at the University of Cape Town.

As he stood there hearing Victor describe and praise Bonelwa, his mind took him back to the first time he met her and the great conversations they used to have, and suddenly, he felt as if he was still in love with her.

"So which one should I wear?" Victor asked.

Tau came back from the past into the present, helped his boss choose what to wear and which cologne to use, and went back to his office. He sat at his desk, deep in thought, asking himself if he had made the biggest mistake of his life by cheating on Bonelwa with Zuki. He thought about many "what ifs", especially if he would have stayed with Bonelwa... would things be better?

While Tau tried to do some work before he left the office, Victor knocked at his door, opened the door enough to let his head in, thanked him for his help, and told him he was on his way to pick up Bonelwa for their date.

After his boss left, Tau got up from his chair and moved across his office and back, saying to himself, "She is not into him. I saw her eyes, she still loves me; not some old bald man. I was her first, she will not forget me. This is just temporary; she will soon understand that Victor is not the one for her."

He left the office feeling worse than when he got there.

CHAPTER FIFTEEN

The following day, Tau arrived early and went straight to his office. He didn't want to hear any details from his boss about his date with Bonelwa the night before. His heart was restless, so he buried himself in his work. He didn't want to entertain any thoughts of Victor and Bonelwa making out; it was just too painful for him to bear.

Though he tried to focus on his work, his mind kept on taking him back to Bonelwa. He recollected the good times he'd had with her. Now that Zuki was so busy with the baby, and didn't have much time for him, he longed for one more embrace with Bonelwa. But his conscience refused to entertain that and brought him back to his situation, reminding him that he had made his choice and that he was now a husband and father.

After an intense battle between his carnal desires and his conscience, he decided to take his lunch break fifteen minutes early, to avoid bumping into his boss or any of his co-workers. He was not in a mood for any kind of chit-chat.

At the corridor, he pressed the lift button to go down. The lift door opened at his floor, and there was Bonelwa, all alone, coming down from Victor's office on the top floor.

"Hi…" Tau greeted.

"Hello Tau," she replied.

As the lift went down, Tau opened his mouth many times, but words wouldn't come out. The scent of her perfume was killing him with the desire to hold her and kiss her passionately, but his conscience kept him put. Bonelwa was texting on her phone the whole time the lift was going down; she didn't pay much attention to him.

The lift beeped to notify them that they had arrived at their destination, which was the ground floor where the exit was.

"We need to talk," Tau said before the door opened.

"Talk about what?" she replied, her eyes fixed on her phone and not giving him any attention.

The lift door opened, and they both went out.

"We need to talk about us; we never really had a chance to talk after all that happened," he replied, looking down.

"Maybe, it's because there was, and still is, nothing to talk about, Tau," she replied and headed on her way.

"Bonelwa, please… let me buy you a cup of coffee… that's all I am asking." Tau walked after her and gently grabbed her by the elbow.

She turned to him and looked at him in distress, her heart yearned for him but her pain said no! She looked him in the eyes and said, "Tau… I don't think it's a good idea."

"It is just a cup of coffee, Baby… sorry, that was a slip of the tongue. What I meant to say is, what harm could a cup of coffee do?"

She looked him in the eyes again. Tau could not bear her piercing eyes, so he looked away. Her heart said yes, but her conscience didn't approve. She ignored the warning from her conscience, but promised to look after herself and protect the pieces of her shattered heart from being further broken.

"I suppose a cup of coffee would not hurt. Let's meet at Brazed Café after work, but you have to drop me home after that because I will miss my lift."

"That's a deal. I'll be there after work, thanks!"

"Okay, I'll see you later, Tau." She left and went back to work.

Later that day, they met at Brazed Café. They sat opposite each other at a table in the back of the restaurant. Tau rubbed his hands under the table, he looked for words that would best express what he was feeling at that very moment, while Bonelwa skimmed through the menu and found what she wanted to order.

She looked at him and said, "I am ready to order. What are you having?"

"I don't know, what do you suggest?" Tau replied.

"They have your favourite pizza, and they do it better than the ones in Cape Town."

"Okay, I trust your judgment, I'll have that then," Tau said.

"Okay," Bonelwa called the waiter over and place their orders.

A few moments later, the waiter returned with their drinks. He served Tau a glass of red wine and Bonelwa a glass of fresh cocktail juice.

Bonelwa took a sip and said, "So what is it that you wanted us to talk about?"

"I have been thinking about the right words to best convey what I really want to say to you since we've arrived here, and yet I still have none," Tau replied.

"Just speak what is in your heart that is what you really want to say. Your mind may want to put things in a way that it thinks is acceptable, but if you really want to say what is in your heart, you must say it without thinking. The greatest truths are always spoken at the slip of the tongue," she encouraged him to talk.

"I guess you're right... the thing is, after all that happened, we never really had a chance to talk things out," he said.

"I agree with you, but I guess it was better that way. I was so angry with you, I don't think I would've listened to anything you would've said at the time," she said.

"Yes, you're right... but how are you holding up?" he asked, his eyes fixed on hers.

"I'm fine," she responded and turned her eyes away.

"Come on, Babe..." he restrained himself, once again, from calling her "Baby".

"Bonelwa, I know you too well, you don't have to pretend with me. This talk is long overdue. I want us to lay everything on the table and take that crucial first step toward healing. So how are you really doing?" he continued.

"I am... I am in pain, Tau," she said, tears rolling down her cheeks. "I am trying my best to pick up the broken pieces of my shattered heart... but it is so hard..." She wiped the tears from her eyes.

Tau offered her his handkerchief, she wiped her tears and said, "Thanks."

She then looked at him, and Tau looked down.

"I was not ready for this... I mean... I was not prepared to lose you, it never crossed my mind. It caught me completely off guard, that's why it threw me off so hard. I know it was naïve of me... but I really believed you when you promised to marry me! What I felt for you was not some young girl infatuation, I really loved you, Tau! And I could feel in my soul that you loved me too; that is why I still cannot understand why this happened. We didn't fight. We were not angry with each other, yet I leave for four days... and when I come back... you've fallen out of love with me... why, Tau, why?" she said, holding back her tears.

"I'm so sorry for all that I have done to you. Please forgive me for all the pain and hurt that I've caused you, and for making you break your promise to your mother. Please forgive me for not keeping my promise that I made to you... every time I see you, my heart is filled with guilt and regret. On the day that my son was born, you know what was the first thing that came into my mind when I saw him the first time? 'This was supposed to be me and Bonelwa.' I am happy, but the cost of my happiness is too heavy for me to bear. I have destroyed your life and I can't carry on like I have done nothing wrong. I need your forgiveness. I need you to forgive me. And perhaps I can learn to forgive myself one of these days, will you forgive me?" Tau begged.

"Oh Tau... I am not going to lie to you... I resent you and Zuki. I want the two of you to pay, and suffer excruciating pain, for what you have done and put me through. I want to personally cast both of you into hell and watch you burn... that's how much I hate you both," she confessed.

"And we deserve that and much more," Tau intercepted.

"Let me finish... even though I hate you and I so badly want to avenge myself on you... I forgive you, Tau... and Zuki too."

"Thank you, Bonelwa... thank you! You've no idea what your forgiveness means to me," Tau thanked her, his eyes swollen with tears, "I know I have made my bed of spikes and I have to lay on it, and I am ready to lay on it as long as I live; but let it be without this heavy guilt that I've been carrying that keeps on pressing me down on my bed of spikes and makes my heart restless—even when I am supposed to be happy," he continued.

"I have to forgive you; if it's not for the two of you, I must do it for myself. This burden is too heavy for me… it has changed me… my gentle heart… I have become something that I am not… I just want to be me again," she said.

"And I believe you can be the Bonelwa I once knew," Tau agreed.

"I know that the pain and the hurt will not just go away… but I am going to take one day at the time and allow my heart to heal. Who knows? Maybe I will find someone that will love me enough to keep his promises to me," she said.

"No one deserves it more than you do, Bonelwa," he affirmed her.

Their conversation was interrupted by the waiter with their food.

As they began to eat, she looked at him and smiled. Her eyes became brighter and she said, "I feel much better, as if a heavy weight has been lifted off my shoulders."

"I am glad to hear that," Tau replied.

As the mood changed, Tau looked at her bright eyes and the glow on her face and said, "There is another reason that I wanted us to talk."

"Okay, I'm all ears. What is it?" she replied.

"That day when you found me in Victor's office, before you came, he went on and on about how great you are. I didn't know whom he was talking about, until you came into the office. Hearing him describe you, reminded me of why I fell in love with you in the first place. I left his office jealous of him being with you. When I got to my office, I couldn't stop thinking about you. I felt the urge to be with you and hold you tight and never let you go out of my sight. The next day I was so afraid to hear him say… you know… that the two of you had… you know… and since that day I can't get you out of my mind. I know… I know… I am married and I have no right to be jealous of you, let alone miss you… but that is just how I feel at this stage," Tau confessed.

"I can relate to that. Most of the time I am enraged at you, but there are times when I hear a song, watch a program, visit places and eat certain foods, that remind me of you; and at the very moment I miss you and I wish you were with me. I guess it happens to all of us," she also confessed.

They talked more as they ate, their gloomy night began to turn into a delightful one as they recalled how they met, their first date, first kiss and the things they used to do together. They made each other laugh out loud and often their eyes locked for a good while until they both blushed.

After they finished their dessert, she suggested they call it a night and asked him to drop her home. Tau asked the waiter for the bill and after paying, they left the restaurant at ten o'clock and headed to Bonelwa's place. It was a fifteen-minute drive.

They arrived at her place and in the parking lot, before she got out of the car, she glanced at him and said, "Thank you for the lift; it was the best night I've had in a long time."

He glanced back at her and replied, "It's my pleasure. I really had a great time. Thank you for forgiving me, you've set my suffocating heart free."

"Don't mention it, maybe I was setting my own self free too," she responded.

After a brief silence, Tau asked, "Who do you stay with in here?"

"Alone, why?" she replied.

"By yourself?" he asked.

"Yes, why are you so surprised? You know that I love my space and sharing is not really my thing," she replied. "Anyway, it is late. I need to rest and you still have to drive a long way."

"Okay, but let me walk you to the door. I want to see you get in and lock the door. I don't want to drive home worrying if you got into your apartment safe or not," he suggested. He got out of the car and opened her door to let her out, and they headed to the doorway of the building. When they got there, she said, "I stay on the first floor. If you don't mind we can take the stairs."

"I don't mind."

They got to the first floor and walked down the corridor.

"This is it for me," she said. She fished out her keys from her handbag, opened her door, got in, turned and said, "Thank you for everything, Tau, it was lovely. Please drive home safely, and let me know once you are home safe. I don't want to worry and lose my sleep."

She tried to close the door, but he blocked it with his left foot. He projected his body toward her to steal a kiss, but she blocked him with both hands resting on his chest and said, "Tau... please."

He ignored her plea and pressed forward. One thing led to another, landing Tau inside her apartment. Tau kicked the door with his left heel and the door closed behind them. They moved toward the bedroom door, when they got to the bedroom door.

"Wait... wait..." she said, trying to catch her breath. "Please give me a second... I was not expecting anyone to enter my room today..." she said, her voice sounding out of breath. "Please... wait here... I will be back in a second," she said and got into her room, shutting the door behind her.

A few minutes later, she opened the door to let him in. He got inside the room and closed the bedroom door behind him.

When their passion had subsided, after a few exchanges of endearment, Tau fell asleep.

However, when all the excitement cooled off and Tau started snoring, Bonelwa lay on her bed staring at the ceiling as tears rolled down her face.

She knocked him with her elbow, and said, "Tau?"

There was no answer.

"Tau!" She hit him again.

Tau tossed and turned, but there was still no answer.

Then, with great force, she hit him in his ribs with her elbow and called, "Tau!"

"Ouch! What was that for?" he complained.

"Tau... are you awake?" she asked.

"Yes, what is it?" he asked.

"Please get up and go home," she said.

"I'll go tomorrow, it's late," he refused.

"Tau... please get up and go back to your wife and son..." she insisted.

"Please let me sleep, I'm tired. I'll deal with them tomorrow," he said and covered his head.

"Tau!!!" Bonelwa shouted. She got out of the bed, put on her robe, and said, "Please go home, Tau..."

"Are you serious?" he asked.

"Please… just leave… please Tau…" she pleaded, tears rolling down her face.

When he saw the tears on her face, he said, "Okay… sorry… I'm leaving… did I do something wrong?"

"No Tau, you did nothing wrong… but I did. Please let me know when you've arrived home safely," she replied.

"Okay," he agreed and went out of her apartment.

She closed the door, leaned against it and slid down to the floor, and with tears said, "What have I done?"

Half an hour later, Tau arrived home safely and before he got out of the car, he sent Bonelwa a text message, *"I'm home."*

"Okay," she replied.

CHAPTER SIXTEEN

It was one o'clock in the morning when Tau arrived home. He found Zuki waiting for him, sleeping on the couch in the sitting room. She awoke when he opened the door and switched on the light.

She jumped from the couch and ran toward him and hugged him tight.

"Thank God you're fine… I have been worried sick about you!"

"I am fine, Sweetheart," he replied.

When she hugged him, a strange scent of perfume assaulted her nostrils. Zuki sniffed him without him being aware, wanting to make sure that it was indeed a woman's perfume on him.

"Tau, where have you been? I have been trying to call you since five o'clock this afternoon," she asked and fixed her eyes on his eyes, paying close attention for any cover ups.

"I… I…" he swallowed hard and looked away.

Zuki opened her eyes wide and asked, "Tau, where were you?"

"I… I went for a few drinks with some people I work with and I lost track of time. I'm sorry, I didn't mean to worry you," he lied.

"Tau, don't lie to me… where were you?" she asked, her arms crossed and eyebrows raised.

"It doesn't matter where I was, Zuki. Anyway, I didn't think you would notice if I came home late or not at all," he replied and shrugged his shoulders.

"What's that supposed to mean, Tau?"

"I mean… I am almost an invisible guest in my own house."

"Really? And that is because…?"

"Ever since the baby was born, I've become invisible to you; unless of course I am needed… only then it's, 'Tau, the baby needs this or that, or I need this or that' and when that is done, I'm sent back to my guest corner."

"Tau, are you hearing yourself? It's your own child I am busy taking care of, how can you be jealous of your own child?"

"I am not jealous of my child, but I do feel neglected by you. All you care about these days is the baby. He takes all your time and attention."

"How can you say that, Tau? That is so selfish of you!"

"I am not being selfish. I did not make a baby to take over our lives—I made a baby to be part of our lives."

Zuki looked at him, psychoanalyzing him, as she looked for words to put him in his place.

"Zuki, when last did you kiss me goodbye when I left the house for work? Or given me the welcome kiss you always gave me when I returned home from work? When, Zuki? When?"

Zuki gazed at her husband while he complained; she knew what he was saying was true. She looked down, and for a moment regretted neglecting her husband, and then she gazed back at him and said, "Tau, things changed. It's not just the two of us anymore, we are parents now. You can't expect me to act like it is just the two of us. I let you sleep the whole night, I don't wake you up in the middle of the night when the baby is crying. I deal with it all by myself because I know that you have to wake up early in the morning and go to work. You don't see me complaining, do you?"

"I know that, and I appreciate that, but what about my needs? Who is going to take care of my needs… who, Zuki? The helper? You used to make me lunch to take to work, and that made me feel loved and appreciated; now the helper has to do that for you. What else must the helper do for you before you wake up?"

"Tau, why can't you put your selfish needs aside for a while? Stop whining, and accept that things are different now, and that we have big responsibilities to deal with!"

"I can't Zuki… I can't just put my need to be loved aside for a while. After a long and stressful day at work, I return home expecting to find love and appreciation, is that too much to ask?"

"Oh, I see. Is that your excuse to run into the arms of another woman, instead of coming home and dealing with the situation?"

"What? I don't have time for this. I'm going to sleep, I need to work tomorrow," Tau shouted and walked away, heading to the bedroom.

"And where do you think you're going?" Zuki shouted back.

"To bed."

"There is no way you are going to sleep next to me tonight."

"What?"

"You heard me… and since you're already feeling like a guest, let's make it official, shall we? The guest room is yours until further notice."

"Are you serious?"

"Dead serious."

Tau looked at her for a good while, shook his head and said, "Okay… I just hope you know what you are doing." He headed to the guest room.

"Please take a shower and throw the clothes you're wearing into the trash before you sleep. I don't want you to defile the bed in the guest room, or this house, with that stench of that woman's perfume you've on you," Zuki shouted behind his back.

Tau stopped, smelt his shirt, and Bonelwa's perfume was all over him. His guilty mind decided to give Zuki no answer, as he continued his journey to the guest room. Not wanting to aggravate the situation, he did what Zuki told him to do.

Zuki didn't sleep much that night. Her body kept on tossing and turning, while her mind sought the answer to the big question that troubled her soul—who was the woman that left her perfume on Tau?

She woke up early, made him lunch, and went to the guest room to take him fresh clothes to wear. She found Tau taking a shower in the guest room. She put the clothes on the bed and noticed Tau's phone on the bed. She looked around at the bathroom door and heard Tau singing while he showered. She went through his phone and read his messages. She found the message he sent Bonelwa, but he'd saved her name has BH. She wrote down the number and left the room.

After the shower, Tau got dressed and went out of the guest room for breakfast. He found Zuki there, making him breakfast.

"Have a seat," she said.

Tau looked puzzled, his mind looking for answers to why she was being so nice to him that morning. Nevertheless, he took a seat and Zuki dished him breakfast and dished for herself as well.

Tau delayed eating, as he looked at the food and looked at Zuki.

Zuki looked at him not eating and said, "Aren't you going to eat? The food is going to get cold and you're going to be late for work." And after saying that, she took a bite and ate some of the food. When Tau saw her eating, he felt a bit more at ease, ate also, and left for work.

Tau spent the whole day thinking about Bonelwa and the great time they'd had together. It reminded him of the great relationship they'd once had.

Bonelwa on the other hand, was having a terrible day. She felt used and blamed herself for what happened. She couldn't wait to go home that day. After work, she went straight to the bus station, greeted Solly, the bus driver, by waving her hands, sat in the back seat, closed her eyes and leaned her head on the seat in front of her.

When she arrived home, she went straight to her bedroom, dropped herself on the bed, and fell asleep.

Two hours later, Tau left the office and rushed to Bonelwa's place. When he arrived there, he knocked on the door, but there was no answer. He kept on knocking until she got out of bed and, with a frown on her face, asked who it was. When Tau replied, she opened the door. Tau wanted to get in, but she blocked him by keeping the door half closed.

"Hey Baby... did you miss me?" Tau asked.

"What are you doing here, Tau?" She asked.

"Baby..."

"Please don't call me that. What do you want from me, Tau?"

"I missed you."

"Last night was a terrible mistake, please go home to your wife and child."

"Why? I want to be with you."

"Because that is where you belong, Tau. Please go now."

"I don't understand, I thought we had a great time yesterday, what happened?"

"I woke up, and realized that it was a big mistake, that's what happened. Can you please leave now, I am not feeling well."

"But..."

"Bye Tau."

She shut the door in his face and leaned her back on it, tears falling down her cheeks.

"Bonelwa, can we please talk about this?" Tau asked from outside.

She wiped her tears and stopped sobbing, so he might not know that she was crying, and answered, "Tau, please don't force me to call security. Please go home to Zuki, please..." Mentioning Zuki's name made her even sadder.

Tau gazed at the closed door and heard her sobbing inside, he put his hand over his face while he stood there quietly. A few moments later, he left.

Bonelwa heard his footsteps as he walked away. Her heart wanted to call him to come back and hold her one last time, but her pain said no. So, she let him go.

She got up and went to her room, opened her laptop and a video file, and was about to hit the delete button, when her phone rang. She looked at the screen and it was an unknown number.

"Hello," she answered, but there was no answer, just heavy breathing and sighing.

"Hello… hello? Who is this? It is not funny. If you don't talk in the next few seconds, I will hang up and not answer your call again," she warned.

"I can't believe this. You just couldn't leave him alone, could you?" the caller replied.

"Zuki, is that you?"

"Yes! When are going to accept that he chose me over you? He's just using you. When he comes to his senses, he'll leave you again," Zuki said.

"How did you get my number?" Bonelwa asked.

"My husband sent you a text message at a very odd hour… and you left your stinking perfume on his clothes."

"Zuki, please address your concerns with your husband and leave me out of this."

"You leave my husband the hell alone and I will stop calling, you little slut."

"Zuki, I am going to give you one more chance. Please hang up the call now and I will forget that you've called and insulted me."

"You've got some nerve… you seduced my husband and you have the nerve to give me an ultimatum! You little…, stay the hell away from my husband!"

"Listen here, Ms. Boyfriend Snatcher, your husband came to me—and yes, we had great sex last night. And today, he came for more but I felt sorry for you and sent him back home. Maybe I should've kept him for tonight also, are you happy now?"

"You… little slut."

"Zuki, last warning. Please hang up the phone and talk things through with your husband—he should be arriving home anytime now."

"Slut, whore, tramp and dirty little girl, leave my husband the hell alone!"

"Okay, that's it, you've asked for it," Bonelwa said and hung up the phone.

"Hello? Hello? You…" Zuki said, after Bonelwa hung up on her.

Just then Tau entered the house.

"Hi Sweetheart, I missed you," Tau said, as he moved toward Zuki to kiss her. But, she turned his kiss away.

"Is everything alright?" he asked.

"You tell me," Zuki replied and crossed her arms.

"What is this all about, Zuki?"

"Tau, please don't play dumb with me, you know what you've done."

"Done what?"

"Okay, please go to your room before I do something crazy and regret it."

Tau took the opportunity and went straight to the guest room and locked the door behind him.

The following day, he woke early and left the house way before his normal time because he wanted to avoid Zuki.

Around ten o'clock in the morning, the buzzer rang at their house. The helper went to see who it was, and she found the courier guy with a package. He asked the helper to call Zuki, or he would take the package back with him.

The helper went to call Zuki, who came and signed for the package, and the courier guy handed her the envelope stamped private and confidential.

Zuki looked at the envelope and walked back to her room. She sat on her bed and opened the envelope. It was a DVD without cover or label, there was just a note that said, *"Watch me."* She put the DVD on and pressed play. As the DVD played, she dropped the remote control that she held in her hands, and with her mouth opened and tears rolling down her face, she watched Tau and Bonelwa having sex.

That night, when Bonelwa had told Tau to wait in the lounge while she fixed up her bedroom, she had set up a hidden video camera to record them having sex, in order to use it as a revenge weapon against Tau and Zuki. But she had changed her mind and was about to delete the video from her laptop and destroy the tape, when Zuki called and insulted her. She then went ahead with her plan and sent it to Zuki via a courier.

After the sex tape ended, there was a video message that Bonelwa recorded for Zuki. Zuki watched as Bonelwa came on her TV screen saying:

"Zuki, you should've taken my warnings seriously. Believe it or not, I was about to delete the tape when you called and insulted me.

I hope now you know how it feels to be betrayed by someone that you trust. I hope you've enjoyed the video.

By the way, if I were you, I wouldn't keep this video for too long. You know it can destroy your husband's dream of becoming Attorney General one day."

Zuki switched off the TV, sat next to her son and gazed upon him with tears falling down her face.

When Tau arrived home that day, he found the DVD on the top of the bed. He put it on and stood there with his hands over his head, saying, "Oh my God... oh my God... I can't believe she did this."

He took his phone and called Bonelwa, but she ignored all his calls. He then decided to go see Zuki. He knocked on the door and said, "Sweetheart, can I come in?"

"Tau, please go away, I don't want to see your face right now. I just hope it was worth it," Zuki responded, crying.

Tau put his hands over his face, then over his head, and walked away to the guest room.

CHAPTER SEVENTEEN

A few weeks later, Zuki, with the help of her father-in-law, succeeded in getting a restraining order against Bonelwa, which prohibited her from coming within ten meters of herself, Tau and her family.

After the restraining order was served, Bonelwa refrained from visiting Victor.

Three days later, Victor called her to find out why she was no longer coming to see him in the office. Bonelwa told him about the restraining order.

Victor didn't take it well. He stood up after he finished talking to Bonelwa and walked to and fro in his office, seeking a solution for the matter. He loved Bonelwa's company and the way she cared for him and how she made him feel alive. Hence, he was not prepared to be deprived of seeing her in his own company. After moving back and forth in his vast office, he sat down when he had decided what to do.

On the following day, he called Tau to his office. When Tau arrived at his boss's office, he found his boss with a grave look.

"Morning, Sir," Tau greeted his boss.

"Morning, Tau," Victor replied. "Please take a seat," Victor told Tau.

"I am sure you are aware that your wife was granted a restraining order against Nelwa," Victor said.

"Yes, Sir, I am well aware of that."

"Tau, I am going to be upfront with you; I like you and you have great potential and a bright future in this firm, but I cannot accept that Nelwa cannot visit me anymore, simply because you work here. You must speak to your wife to re-evaluate the restraining order."

"Yes, Sir, I understand. I'll try to get her to drop the restraining order."

"Tau, please don't try, do it. See Tau, I am old and rich; winning cases and making money are the last things on my mind. I was contemplating retirement because coming to work became such a pain, until I met Nelwa. She injected new life into me and gave me a reason to enjoy and live life to the fullest, for whatever time I've left on this earth. However, I am counting on you to revive this firm, and maybe one day take over it, which is why it would break my heart to let you go."

"Thank you, Sir, I promise I will speak to Zuki as soon I get home."

"Okay, Tau, thank you for understating; that will be all."

"Thank you, Sir."

Tau left Victor's office and went straight to his office to think about what he would do. On his way, he meditated on how to get Zuki to change her mind and drop the restraining order against Bonelwa.

When he arrived home, Zuki welcomed him with a kiss, took off his jacket and got him a drink. Tau wanted to talk but was hesitant; he didn't what to spoil Zuki's efforts to patch things up between them.

After hesitating for a while, he finally got up the courage and called her to the sitting room.

"What's wrong Tau? Why do you look so serious?" Zuki asked.

"Sweetheart, we need to talk," Tau replied.

"What's the matter, Tau?"

"Victor and Bonelwa are somehow close these days, but lately she can't come to the office to see Victor because of the restraining order. Because of that, Victor called me into his office this morning and asked me, to ask you, to reconsider the restraining order."

"And what did you say to him?"

"I said, I'll talk to you."

"Tau, I can't do that. I must protect my family against Bonelwa. I will not allow her to destroy this family; please tell Victor I can't do that."

"Victor made things very clear to me; if you don't do it, I'll lose my job."

"He can't just fire you like that."

"Actually, he can. He owns sixty-five percent of the firm, and the other shareholders owe him their shares. None of them would stick out their necks for me; besides, some of them see me as a threat to their ambitions in the firm."

"That snake! She won't leave us alone!"

"You don't have to do it if you are not comfortable with it. I can just resign."

"Yes, maybe it's time for you to work for your dad. You don't need Victor and his little slut."

"I can't work for my dad."

"Why not, Tau?"

"I went to law school to help people get justice, not to defend some rich criminals, who think they're above the law and their money can buy their way out of prison after committing a crime."

"What are you going to do then?"

"I will apply for a job at the Attorney General's office."

"Okay, that is a good idea, Tau."

The following day, Tau went to Victor's office and told him that Zuki refused to drop the restraining order.

Victor looked at Tau and then looked down and said, "I am sorry, Tau, but I've got to let you go then. But I don't want to fire you, it would be better if you resign. I'll gladly write a letter of recommendation."

"Thank you, Sir, I appreciate it."

Tau left Victor's office, tendered his resignation, went to his office and packed all his belongings, and left the office.

Victor looked at Tau carrying the box with his belongings through his office window and sighed, his countenance fallen. His eyes followed Tau until he was out of sight. He took his phone and called Bonelwa.

"Hello Nelwa," Victor greeted.

"Hi Victor," Bonelwa greeted back.

"I've got good news for you," Victor announced.

"Really? What is it?" Bonelwa asked, excited.

"I just asked Tau to resign. He resigned and left the office, so you are now free to visit me at any time."

"What? That is terrible news! Why did you fire him, Victor? He has a wife and baby to look after; you should not have fired him."

"I thought you would be happy."

"No, Victor, I am not. This is bad news and it has just spoiled my day, I never asked you to do that for me."

"Yes, Nelwa, I know that, but I thought I was removing the stumbling block from our friendship."

"Okay Victor, I have to go now; we'll talk some other time."

"Okay Nelwa, call me, okay?"

"Bye, Victor."

"Bye, Nelwa."

Bonelwa hung up and Victor held the handset off the hook in deep thought about Bonelwa's reaction to his news.

A few weeks passed without Victor and Bonelwa seeing each other. She didn't just refuse to come to his office but also avoided his calls, which left Victor desperate.

On a Monday morning, Victor decided to pay Bonelwa a visit at the bank. She came out to see him and he pleaded with her to have coffee with him, and she agreed.

On her lunch break, they went for lunch at the restaurant where they first met.

While they were eating, Bonelwa gazed at Victor with a childlike look and said,

"Please give Tau his job back."

"I've tried to do that for the past two weeks, but he got a job at the Attorney General's office. Apparently, one of their lawyers joined a private firm and left a vacancy, and Tau got it."

"Okay, that's great news! I feel better now."

After lunch they both headed to their respective work places.

They continued to spend time with each and became really close.

On a long weekend, Victor desperately wanted to move out from the friend zone into something much more, so he decided to ask

Bonelwa to spend the weekend with him in Zanzibar, and to put her at ease. He promised to book separate rooms for each of them, and Bonelwa agreed.

In Zanzibar, they were having a great time; Victor showered Bonelwa with many expensive gifts and to his surprise she accepted them. Things got cosier between them with each moment that they spent together.

On Saturday night, after returning from a party at the hotel, they found themselves in Victor's room. Victor made his move and tried to kiss Bonelwa, but she gently pushed him away and said, "I can't do this, Victor."

"Why not?" asked Victor in despair.

"Because you're married; I cannot do this to your wife, nor to me."

Victor sat on the edge of the bed while he heard her giving him her reasons why she put the brakes on that intimate moment.

It was the last thing he wanted to hear, but he respected her decision. When she was done talking, she left his room and went to sleep in her own room.

They left the Zanzibar on Monday, after landing, he dropped her at her place and went home. They didn't talk much on the way.

Two days later, Bonelwa bought Victor a healthy lunch and went to see him at his office. Victor was glad to see her.

She pulled up a chair and looked at him for a good while without saying a word, until he blushed and looked down.

"What?" Victor asked.

"Can I ask you a few personal questions?" she asked.

"Yes, go ahead."

"Do you love your wife?"

"Yes, I do."

"Does your wife love you?"

"Yes, she does."

"Why then do you betray her love like that, running around with young girls like me?"

"I honestly don't know; maybe it is lust or maybe I just want to be intimate with someone and feel alive again."

"And why are you not intimate with your own wife?"

"I guess we are too used to each other and we have lost that special connection we used to have."

"You've helped me to stay out jail, and I can help you connect with your wife again, if you let me."

"Okay, I would like that. After what happened at the hotel and the things you said there, it got me thinking a lot about it. I don't want to betray my wife anymore, and I would really appreciate your help."

"Okay, it's a deal then… but you have to do exactly what I tell you, agreed?

"Agreed."

They shook hands and Bonelwa went back to work.

The following weeks Bonelwa spent a lot of time with Victor, helping him to lose weight, eat healthily, and buying his wife flowers, cards and gifts.

After six weeks, Victor told her that he and his wife had become intimately involved again, and he thanked her.

~* ~* ~* ~

Four months after the trial, Tshepo Mafoko awoke from his coma and began to recover.

CHAPTER EIGHTEEN

As time went by, Bonelwa moved from one relationship to another; not because they were unsuccessful, but because she ended most of them when she saw the relationship was getting serious. She wanted to protect her heart. Breaking up with others gave her a sense of being in control, rather than waiting for others to break up with her; that way, she felt she was the one that left the relationship, and thus the one in control.

Among some of the people that she dated, there were two that almost had her going all the way with the relationship.

One of them was Fumani, a high school English teacher. Fumani was like the male version of Bonelwa. They were so compatible and shared so many similar traits that it scared both of them. They were both avid readers. They read almost the same books, had the same aspirations in life, and they could speak about fiction characters for hours, as if they were real people.

After six months of dating, on a hot summer day, while they were reading a classical book neither had ever read before, Fumani bowed to his knee, took a one carat diamond engagement ring from his pocket, and gazed into Bonelwa's eyes. With his eyes full of love and passion he said, "Bonelwa Hlazo, will you marry me?" Bonelwa's eyes gazed at him, as she didn't know what to say. Tears poured from her eyes, while she gazed upon him. Then she closed her book, wiped her tears with her hands and said, "I am sorry, Fumani, I am not ready for this. I'm so sorry, I've got to go." She grabbed all her belongings and dashed off—and that was the end of their promising relationship.

The other one was Isaac Moloto, a news anchor at a TV station.

He was good-looking, smart and fun, and he loved Bonelwa with everything in him. He almost worshiped the ground that she walked on. So strong and real was his love that she could feel it in her shattered heart.

On Bonelwa's twenty-fourth birthday, Isaac organized a surprise party for her at his house. Isaac picked up Bonelwa from work and drove her to his place. When she entered the house, she was greeted by a loud shout from some friends, "Surprise!" They all shouted at once. Her eyes brightened up and she said, "Thank you all, I really appreciate this, it means a lot to me."

The party began and they were all having a great time, until they were interrupted by the DJ for everyone to give their gifts to the birthday girl. One by one they handed their gifts to her, leaving only Isaac to hand over his gift. Isaac asked the DJ for the mic and said, "Before the birthday girl cuts the cake, I want to give this beautiful woman, whom I love with my very life, a special gift."

He then approached her and bowed to his knee, took out a five carat engagement ring and said, "You are the most beautiful woman I've seen, and I love you more than I love myself; Bonelwa, will you marry me?"

Bonelwa looked at him and the people around them, holding their breath in anticipation of her answer, and replied with her mouth almost closed, "Yes." She stretched out her left hand and Isaac placed the ring on her ring finger. Isaac got up and asked for the champagne prepared for the occasion, and they served the people and they toasted to their love. They partied until four o'clock in the morning; some left, while others remained behind to continue the celebration.

Bonelwa spent the next two days avoiding Isaac; on the third day after their engagement, she agreed to meet with him after work. They met at a restaurant opposite her apartment.

They sat opposite each other facing away from each other. Isaac took courage and stretched his hand across the table and said,

"Are you okay, Honey?"

"Yes, I am fine, thanks. And you?"

"I'm confused; I don't know how I am."

"I am so sorry for giving you false hope. I wanted to say no, but I didn't want to embarrass you in front of all those people; that is why I said a very cold 'yes'—I hoped you'd pick it up."

"I don't understand, did I do something wrong?" Isaac asked, his eyes almost pouring tears.

"No, Isaac, you've done everything right, the problem is not with you, it's with me. I am not ready for marriage."

"It's okay, Bonelwa, I can wait until you are ready."

"I can't let you put your life on hold for something that might never happen. You deserve better."

"I deserve better?" Isaac shouted. "You are the better, Bonelwa, and I deserve you!"

"I am really sorry Isaac, I don't know what's wrong with me," she said in tears.

"Then let's get someone to help you deal with whatever is troubling you."

"I don't think it's that simple, Isaac. I'm afraid to be loved, I'm afraid of commitment when it comes to relationships. I guess I fear it will eventually end and I'll be left heart-broken again."

"I'll never hurt you, Bonelwa, I promise."

"I know, Isaac. My fear is not just about you hurting me; what if I cannot love you, the way you love me, and I hurt you?"

Bonelwa's question got both of them thinking and doing a bit of self-introspection.

They left the restaurant without officially breaking up, but they both knew that it was the end of their relationship.

CHAPTER NINETEEN

On the fourth of September of the following year was Bonelwa's twenty-fifth birthday. She was not dating anyone at the time and with her family living in another province, she decided to take herself out and celebrate her birthday alone.

She booked a table for one at a fancy restaurant to spoil herself on her special day. When she arrived at the restaurant the place was packed; it was a Friday and many people were celebrating their birthdays that day.

A waiter escorted her to a table and she placed her order. While the waiter went to get Bonelwa her favourite sparkling juice, she took out her favourite book, with intention to take a quick trip to wonderland on her birthday, while she waited for her drink and food. A few minutes later, the waiter returned with her drink and promised to bring the food shortly after.

Because it was the restaurant's tradition to offer small birthday cakes to its patrons celebrating their birthdays in the restaurant, the waiter brought her food with a complimentary small birthday cake with lit candles shaped in number twenty-five. He was accompanied by his fellow waiters, and together they sang "Happy Birthday" to her. Bonelwa's eyes radiated with pleasure at her waiter's gesture, and thanked him for his efforts in making her special day a delightful day. After she blew out the candles, the waiters left her table and went about doing their duties.

Left alone, she was reminded that she was celebrating her twenty-fifth birthday alone. She looked around and saw people celebrating their birthdays with their families, friends, boyfriends and girlfriends, and her eyes dimmed and became swollen with tears; she felt all alone and out of place. And to make the situation worse, once it became known that it was her birthday, because of the waiters' performance at her table, some of the patrons in the restaurant started to peek at her from time to time, especially a group of five young women who were celebrating their friend's birthday. They kept on gazing at her and then they would laugh among themselves.

Bonelwa was only half way through her meal, but she couldn't take anymore, seeing people celebrating their birthdays with their loved ones and the mocking of the young girls, she decided to call it a night and asked her waiter for a doggy bag for her meal and the cake, then she asked him to bring the bill as well.

The waiter cleared her table and a few minutes later, he returned with the doggy bag and the bill. She thanked him and paid the bill in cash, tipping her waiter half the bill; the waiter's eyes almost popped out when he saw his tip and thanked her profusely. She left the restaurant with her head down and went straight home.

When she arrived at her apartment, she kicked her high heels away, sighed and dropped herself on the couch, her head down and teared up.

"What's wrong with me?" she asked herself, her hands covering her face and making her hands wet with bitter tears. She turned on her side with her hands covering her face and fell asleep out of sorrow.

Her sleep was disturbed by a strange beep; she turned the other way and ignored the beep. A few moments later it beeped again.

"Ahrrrr!" She murmured and got up, walking toward the table where the phone that Victor gave her during her court case was beeping. It was a text message from Victor:

> *"Thank you very much, Nelwa. I love my wife more than ever. I was a fool for neglecting and betraying my wife, but she forgave me. We went to Mauritius to renew our vows, and it is all thanks to you. Thank you, you've saved my marriage. I hope all works out for you too... take care."*

"Good for you, Victor. I hope so too, but right now my life is messed up."
She replied.
"I'm sorry to hear that. Hang in there, love might just surprise you!"
He replied.
"I wish I shared your enthusiasm. Anyway, let me not spoil your happiness with my whining. Thanks for everything Victor, enjoy."

She then switched off the phone, got up to get a knife, sat on the couch, cut a piece of her birthday cake with her right hand, grabbed the remote control with her left hand, and turned on the TV. A romantic movie was on at that moment, so she flipped the channel and a couple was kissing on that channel, she flipped again and a talk show was on. And before she could change it, the host said, "Are you single, lonely and in search of your perfect match? Do you want to meet the love of your life? If your answer to those two question is yes, then you need to come to our studios this Saturday… and who knows? You might just return home hooked up with the love of your life. And if you meet your perfect one, we'll feature you on the show. Don't forget, tomorrow morning at nine o'clock, we'll be hosting a Meet & Mingle breakfast. Seats are limited, so book yours now to avoid disappointment. Go to our website now and fill out the online form to reserve your place.

"This is Perfect Match, you too, deserve to be loved!"

"Yea… right. Too cheesy to be true—that should be your slogan!" She retorted at the TV host.

She continued to watch as the show advertised couples that met through the show, some couples giving their testimony on how they met.

She sat there and stared at the ceiling, weighing her options.

"What the hell, I've got nothing to lose," she said and got up to get her laptop from the bedroom. She logged on to the website and filled out the online form.

Two hours later, she received an email confirming her seat for the event.

Early on the following day, she put on her favourite dress and rushed to attend the event. The guest speaker was a famous talk show host and a relationship coach. After the keynote address, they were led to a different hall where they were to have breakfast. At the door, they were escorted by ushers and sat according to the list arrangements, which was five men and five women seated at a round table that accommodates ten people.

As the event progressed and "Perfect Matches" began to be put together, most of the serious people who came with the hope of finding someone special, quickly realized that the producers of the show were more interested in getting people to appear on their show than to help people find love, so they left the studio upset. The producers went along with those who were desperate to appear on TV and put on a good show of being "in love" in order to have their stint of fame.

When Bonelwa saw the fake couples playing in love for the cameras, she left, disappointed. She decided to go to a park nearby and read. On her way to the park, she got tired of walking in high heels, so she took them off and carried them in her hands, walking barefoot.

When she arrived at the park, she sat on a bench next to a lake and read. While she read, she heard a child running and laughing as he ran. She took her eyes off the book and looked at the child, as he ran to his father to be picked and lifted up high into the air. When the father picked up and tossed him into the air, Bonelwa realized that the father playing with his son was Tau, and next to them was Zuki, with their baby girl.

She watched them from afar, while they played and seemed so happy together. It was all she had ever wanted. Tears rolled down her face as she continued to watch the happy family play and enjoy themselves.

She wiped her tears, grabbed all her belongings and left the park, promising herself to forgive and leave Tau and Zuki alone for good. She held back her tears on her way to the bus station, while she wondered:

"What did I do to deserve this? Why can't I be loved? Why can't someone love me in a way that I am not afraid to get hurt again? Will I ever find lasting love?"

"God loves you!" Shouted the street preacher, as Bonelwa passed him by.

Bonelwa looked at him perplexed, wondering why he said that.

"The Word of God says in John chapter three, verse sixteen: 'For God so loved the world that He gave His only begotten Son, that whoever believes in Him should not perish but have everlasting life.'

Miss, God loves you so much that he gave His Son Jesus to die for you," the street preacher said approaching her.

"Do you have a minute, Miss?" he asked.

Bonelwa rolled her eyes and gave the preacher a look that said, "Just say whatever you want to say, so that we both can go our separate ways."

"I feel compelled in my spirit to tell you that Jesus loves you," the preacher said.

"I doubt that, Sir," Bonelwa retorted.

"Why do you say that?" the preacher asked.

"I just don't see any evidence of God's love in my life. On the contrary, I think God is angry at me, in fact, I have a lot of evidence that proves that God is angry with me," Bonelwa replied.

"I doubt that, Miss. You may be angry or indifferent toward God, but God is not angry or indifferent toward you. God loves you so much that He died for your sins; He is just waiting for you to realize how much He really loves you," the preacher insisted.

"Really? Are you saying that with all the things I've done, and trust me, I've done a lot of bad things… are you saying God still loves me?" Bonelwa asked the preacher.

"Yes, that's what I'm saying… it does not matter who you are, where you are from, or what you have done—God loves you! And He wants you to come to the knowledge of His love for you and be saved.

"Do not worry, Miss, about what you have done or said or thought, for there is nothing you have done, said or thought, that has not been done, said and thought before.

"Everything that you have done has been done by someone else before you, and some of these people have now accepted God's offer of forgiveness, so all that they have ever done, God has forgiven them. And not only that, God has also forgotten all their sins!

"The word of God says, that none of us is righteous, we are all saved by the mercy and kindness of God. It says right here in Titus chapter three, verses three through seven:

"'For we ourselves [that is, all of us, who have now accepted God's offer of forgiveness] were also once foolish, disobedient, deceived, serving various lusts and pleasures, living in malice and envy, hateful and hating one another. But when the kindness and the love of God our Saviour toward man appeared, not by works of righteousness which we have done, but according to His mercy He saved us, through the washing of regeneration and renewing of the Holy Spirit, whom He poured out on us abundantly through Jesus Christ our Saviour, that having been justified by His grace we should become heirs according to the hope of eternal life.'

"And you too, Miss, can be forgiven by God today, this very hour! All you have to do is to receive Jesus Christ as your Lord and personal Savior."

"I'm sorry, Sir, I would love to chat more with you, but that's my bus approaching," Bonelwa said, pointing at the bus approaching the bus station.

"Okay, Miss… thank you for your time… here is a little booklet for you to read on the bus on your way home," the preacher said.

"Thank you, Sir," Bonelwa replied, took the booklet and moved on to the bus station.

She waited at the bus station to catch the bus home. A few seconds later the bus arrived. She got on the bus and greeted Solly, the bus driver, on her way to take a seat. She looked out the window and saw the preacher, his eyes fixed on her, following her as the bus departed, until she could see him no more.

The bus dropped her in front of her apartment.

She entered her apartment and kicked her door with her bare heel, slammed it, went straight to bed, took a dive into her bed and slept with her clothes on because taking them off seemed like hard work to her at that moment.

She was awakened when the alarm on her clock radio went off at six o'clock in the morning. She stretched out her hand, without looking, to switch it off, and instead of turning the alarm off, she turned the radio on.

"Relationships are difficult and it requires work from both parties to make it work," said the guest speaker on the radio, getting Bonelwa's attention.

"What about people that have been severely wounded by past relationships and now are afraid to commit, or put in the work, for fear of being disappointed? What advice would you give to our listeners that find themselves in such situations?" the radio host asked the guest speaker.

"The safest way to protect yourself from getting hurt is not to date at all. But the only way to experience true love and a fulfilling relationship, is to open your heart and expose it to love, which is a risky thing to do. A closed heart cannot enjoy love. It doesn't matter how perfect and loving your partner is, if your heart is closed, the relationship will eventually stagnate. Therefore, my advice is to open your heart and let love get in," the guest speaker responded.

"Wow! I think what you've just said may free many of our listeners, who might have closed their hearts because of past hurt. There you have it, 'Open your heart and let love get in' it is that simple. This is Move Radio, 97.8 FM, we will be back after the commercial break, stay tuned," the radio host announced.

Bonelwa sat on her bed and pondered the stranger's words that penetrated her heart and cut to the core of her dilemma—she had shut her heart, that's why love could not get in.

CHAPTER TWENTY

That same day, she got out of her bed with the resolution to open her heart and let love in. So she decided not to stay indoors, wallowing in self-pity, but instead go out to the park and be open to maybe meeting a bookworm, a good-looking and loving man. After taking a long shower, she dressed up and stood in front of the mirror to put on her makeup.

Then she looked at her reflection in the mirror and said, "You're beautiful and, you too, deserve to be loved. Now, open your heart and let love come in. I mean it. I don't want to hear you say, 'What if I get hurt?' You heard the man on the radio, relationships are risky!"

She turned sideways to check out her outfit and then turned her back on the mirror to check out how she looked from behind.

She turned around and faced the mirror, blew a kiss to her reflection, turned sideways again and turned her neck to face the mirror, and said in a James Bond tone, "Nelwa, Bonelwa Hlazo." Then she turned her whole body to face the mirror one more time, did some touch ups on her makeup and hair, and said, "Well, if love is a gamble, I'm ready to play."

She left her apartment and headed for the park next to where she lived.

When she arrived at the park it was a hot sunny day, so she looked for a bench in the shade. She found one but there was an old man already sitting there. She looked around for another bench in the shade but they were all taken, with most of them having more than one person. She took up courage and decided to go to the one where the old man was sitting.

"Hi," she greeted with a wide smile, and waved at the old man.

"Hello, can I help you?" asked the old man.

"I... I... I couldn't find an empty bench in the shade, do you mind if I sit next to you?"

"Why?"

"Oh... I... I just got this new book and I can't wait to delve into it, so I thought, if you don't mind, I could just sit next to you and quietly read it."

The old man looked at her and gave her no answer.

"I promise not to disturb your quiet moment... I'm a quiet reader."

"It's a public park, isn't it?" the old man asked.

"Yes, it is."

"It's a public bench, isn't it?"

"Yes, Sir, it is."

The old man went quiet, in deep thought.

"So can I sit next to you or not?"

"Miss, if you are asking for my permission, you should at least ask in proper English. Which, in this case, should be, 'May I sit next to you?'"

"Oh... I see... *May* I sit next you?"

"Of course you can."

"Isn't your response incorrect? In this case, I was expecting your answer to be, 'Yes, you may sit next to me.'"

"Do you want to sit or not?"

"Yes, of course."

She sat next to the old man, rolling her eyes. She took her book and delved into it.

The old man looked at her, lost into the story, cleared his throat and said, "What are you reading, anyway?"

"It's called Lost and Found. It's a book about a woman that lost her high school sweetheart and found love in the most unexpected place."

"Okay, let me not keep you from your lovely story. Please go on and read your book."

"It's okay, I don't mind at all. I'm Bonelwa," she said and stretched her hand out to shake his.

"Vusi Ndalo. It's a pleasure meeting you, Bonelwa."

"The pleasure is all mine."

"I think you have a fan, who cannot wait for me to leave, but I will make him sweat a little bit more."

"Uhm… I don't get it, what do you mean?"

"Don't look now, but there is a young man seated on the bench to our left, who keeps looking at you with the eyes of love, or lust. Unfortunately, your generation doesn't quite know the difference."

"Okay, thank you for letting me know."

"No problem."

"If you don't mind me asking, what is the difference? I mean, how do you spot the difference between lust and love?"

"It's actually very easy to tell once you learn the difference. The primary objective of love is to give; and the primary objective of lust is to take. And therein lies the difference. When a man really, and I mean really, loves a woman, he gives himself unreservedly to her—his mind, heart, soul, body, attention, time and his wallet—he surrenders it all to the one who has conquered his heart.

"Lust, on the other hand, only wants to take, take and take. It has no interest in giving because lust is selfish and self-centred by nature. Lust only gives when its gain far outweighs its giving.

"When a man loves a woman, he wants to get to know her; what she likes and what she doesn't like, so that he may do what she likes, to make her happy, and avoid doing the things that would make her sad. He envisions building a life with her, therefore, he talks about plans for the future in his conversation.

"When a man lusts after a woman, he wants to get into her pants as soon as he can. All his activities concerning the woman are scheming to get him there as fast as possible. He may even learn what she likes, to better his chance with her. Therefore, his conversation is always about the now, fulfilling his lust. He is allergic to any conversation about the future and building a life together.

"I guess the best way to test him is to bring that up, as soon as you are comfortable with each other. Some people say that scares and chases men away. I doubt that, I believe most men know whether they want to marry the woman or not, after just a few encounters, some even at the first encounter.

"So, if a man is scared and disappears, simply because a woman talked about the future and building a life together, he doesn't deserve the woman, which saves her from wasting her time and effort on something that has no future. At this point, the woman must have the courage to let him go back to his mother, grow up, and come back when he is ready to be a man!"

Bonelwa sat there with her mouth wide open, as her mind processed the wisdom of the strange old man. Then she turned to face the old man and said, "Thank you, I've learned more about love, relationships, and men in these few minutes I've spent with you, than from all the books I've read, and that's a lot. Nobody ever put it so concisely and frankly."

"You're welcome," Vusi said.

While they sat there and talked with each other, Vusi's phone rang.

"Oops… that's my boss, I better run before I'm lashed," Vusi announced.

"Are you still working at this age?" Bonelwa asked.

"Yes, except that this job never ends and I don't get paid any money for doing it. Yet, I work every day, sometimes happy and joyful, other times sad and downcast, but I have to work every day and can't take off until I'm buried under the ground."

"I don't get it… what do you mean, I don't understand?"

"I mean, my boss is my wife and my marriage is my job. She went to shop at the mall and I didn't want to go up and down the mall with her. So, I told my boss she must call me when she is done shopping, and I came here to enjoy the silence and fresh air. Now that she is calling me, I guess she's done."

"Oh… it makes perfect sense… okay, I get it."

While she was still talking, Vusi's phone rang again.

"Bonelwa, it has been a pleasure talking to you. I must leave now, before I upset my boss, but here is my card. You seem like a very bright young woman. If you ever need anything, please call me, and I mean it—and please don't ask me over the phone if you can call me, just call, okay?"

"Okay, I'll hold you to this, Dr. Vusi Ndalo, it was a pleasure talking to you. Now please run before your boss comes to fetch you here."

"Yes, bye."

"Bye, Dr. Ndalo."

The old man called his wife and told her he was on his way to her, as he walked away from Bonelwa toward the mall.

Bonelwa watched the old man as he went, until he was out of sight.

She took her book and delved back into the story she was reading.

Five minutes later, her reading was interrupted by a clearing of the throat.

She took her eyes away from the book, followed the shadow, and faced the guy who was checking her out all along.

"Hi," he said.

"Hi," she said.

"I come here often, but I don't remember seeing you before. Do you come here often, or is it your first time?" he asked.

"Actually, it's my third time."

"Okay, I am Thato, and you are?"

"Bonelwa, but you can call me Nelwa."

"What are you reading?" Thato asked.

"Lost and Found, and you?" Bonelwa replied.

He didn't know the name of the book he was holding, so he showed the book to give himself a chance to read the title himself.

"What is it about?" she asked.

"This and that, you know? Nothing special yet, but I've just started; hope it gets better as it goes," he replied.

"Okay."

They continued to talk and Thato made his moves on her. She was open to love, but now she knew how to differentiate love from lust.

"Thato! Thato! What are you doing there? And why did you take my book? You better bring it back right now, if you know what's good for you!" His five-month pregnant girlfriend shouted.

"Okay, I'll be right there," he shouted back.

"It was nice meeting you, Nelwa, but I have to go now," he said.

"Okay, Thato," she retorted.

"I hope we can see each other again soon… maybe we can go out for drinks?"

"I doubt that. You better go, she is coming this way."

"Thanks, bye."

"Bye, Thato."

Thato walked away and met with his girlfriend on the way. She took the book from his hand and hit him with it on the head.

Bonelwa watched the drama from afar, laughed and said, "Definitely, lust." And she burst into a laugh by herself.

She continued to read, uninterrupted, until it was almost sunset. Then she went to the shops, grabbed something to eat, and went back to her place.

CHAPTER TWENTY-ONE

O
n Monday of the following week, while she helped a client at the bank, the client suddenly switched from business and started making moves on her.

"What time are you knocking-off today? I'll come and pick you up here and take you to this great place I know. I don't know if you've ever been there, but their food is superb. What do you say?"

"Sir, do you realize that I have eyes, and I can see the ring on your finger? What makes you think that I would be interested in going out with a married man?"

"Oh, the ring; this ring thing is overrated and whoever invented it, is a fool. Ring or no ring, people will always step out from the boredom of marriage and get some action outside, before they die of boredom."

"That's your opinion, and I respect that, but as for me, a man with a ring on his finger is a no go zone."

"Will it make a difference if I take it off?"

"Not at all. It is not about the ring itself, but the commitment and vow you made to the person that put the ring on your finger."

The client bounced his lips left and right as he pondered what he had just heard. Then he bounced back and said, "Some take it off when they step out on their partners. Me, I keep it on, I prefer an open policy. It is better that the person knows what she's getting herself into, that way there are no surprises and we both know where we stand. For surely, I am not looking for someone to replace my wife, I love my wife. I'm just looking for someone that understands what I want and they are okay with it, do you get me?"

"Yes, I get you loud and clear. Thank you for your offer and honesty, but I'm going to have to pass. Now, if you no longer have need of my assistance, you must excuse me, Sir, I have to attend to other clients. Thank you for your business."

"Okay, thank you, Miss, you're very kind. I'll see you next time then."

"Thank you. Enjoy the rest of your day, Sir."

"Thank you."

The client left the bank and she proceeded to help the next client in line.

~* ~* ~* ~

Bonelwa's fallout with Zuki made her allergic to friends, let alone best friends. And even though she had been working in the bank for a while, she had never once had a friendly conversation with any of her co-workers. However, among all her co-workers, there was a lady with whom she wouldn't mind being friends. Her name was Lerato. She was the personal assistant to the head of her department, about ten years older than Bonelwa, and she was married. She was always nice to her, but Bonelwa always brushed her off to avoid forming any bond that could develop into a friendship.

On Wednesday of that same week, Lerato came to Bonelwa's desk.

"Hi, Bonelwa," Lerato greeted.

"Hi, Lerato," Bonelwa greeted back.

"The boss lady asked me to give you these documents," Lerato informed Bonelwa.

"Okay. Thank you, Lerato," Bonelwa said.

Lerato handed Bonelwa the documents, turned around and took a few steps to go back to her own desk; then she stopped, turned around, and returned to Bonelwa's desk.

"Do you have any plans for tonight?" Lerato asked.

"No, I don't, why?" Bonelwa replied.

"It's my husband's birthday today, so we're having a braai tonight, nothing big, it will be just us, a few close friends and his younger brother. I would love you to come, that is, if you want to?" Bonelwa looked at Lerato, processing why Lerato invited her, and whether she should go to the braai or not.

"Okay... I would love to come, thank you for inviting me, Lerato," Bonelwa accepted Lerato's invitation.

"Great! You won't regret it, it will be fun. It starts at six o'clock. Here is my address. It is walking distance from where you live, and when you feel like going home, just let me know, I'll drop you off," Lerato said, wrote down her address and handed it to Bonelwa.

"Thank you, Lerato. I'll be there by six o'clock."

"Okay, Bonelwa, I'll see you later then."

Bonelwa left work, went straight to the nearby mall to buy a new summer dress to wear for the braai, and went home to freshen up and went to Lerato's place. At the door, she rang the bell and the door was opened by a very handsome and well-built young man.

"Hi," he greeted

"Hi," Bonelwa replied, and looked away to conceal her instant attraction to him.

His eyes ran to and fro over her body.

"You must be Bonelwa?" he asked.

"Yes, the one and only," she replied and avoided eye contact.

"Come on in. I am Simon, Lerato's brother in law."

"Nice meeting you, Simon."

"The pleasure is all mine," Simon said, as he watched her walk past him and checked her from behind. He closed the door and rushed to show her the way to the yard where the braai was taking place.

"Please follow me this way," he said, as he led her to the yard.

"Thank you."

When Lerato saw Bonelwa, she dropped what she was doing, welcomed and hugged her, and said, "I'm glad you made it."

"Thanks," Bonelwa replied.

"Hello everyone," Lerato announced, "This is my friend Bonelwa, she works with me at the bank.

"Hi, Bonelwa, welcome to our world," they all replied and then introduced themselves to her. They were mostly couples, only Bonelwa and Simon and an old guy were single.

Bonelwa and Simon spent most of their time talking to each other. By the time she left the braai, they had agreed to go on a date on Friday. Lerato played the matchmaker by playing busy and asked Simon to drop Bonelwa home, to which he complied and dropped her home.

Bonelwa went to bed filled with hope. Simon ticked all her boxes, expect that he was not brainy or a bookworm, but she decided she'd be willing to compromise on those, if he was the one for her.

Friday night at six o'clock, Simon came to pick up Bonelwa and took her to an Italian restaurant. At the restaurant they were greeted by a friendly waitress.

"Hi, table for two?" she asked.

"Yes, please," Simon replied.

"Smoking or non-smoking?" the waitress asked.

"Non-smoking, please," Bonelwa replied.

"Please follow me," the waitress requested.

They were seated at one of the tables in the back, and after perusing the menu, they placed their orders. While they drank and ate, Bonelwa quickly realized why Simon was still single. He kept on checking out the lady that was seated at the table in front of them with her boyfriend. And when the lady was flattered with his advances, he was emboldened to wink at her, and she winked back at him. Her boyfriend noticed the wink and so did Bonelwa.

"What the hell are you winking at?" asked the lady's boyfriend as he turned around and saw Simon making gestures at his girlfriend. He got up and walked to their table, looked at Simon, and said, "Wink one more time at my girlfriend, and you'll see what will happen to those pretty eyes of yours."

Simon shrank in fear and gave him no answer. The guy left and went back to his table. Bonelwa looked down and said, "Oh no, lust again."

"What? I didn't get what you just said," Simon asked.

"Nothing, can we just finish and go? It's getting late," Bonelwa replied.

Bonelwa lost her appetite and waited for Simon to finish his food. When he was done, Bonelwa asked the waitress for the bill.

When she returned with it, she put it next to Simon, who checked his pocket and said, "I can't believe this, I forgot my wallet at my brother's place, do you mind taking care of the bill? I promise, I'll pay you back as soon I get my wallet."

Bonelwa shook her head and said, "Fine." She settled the bill and said, "Can we please go now?"

"Yes, we can go."

On their way home, Simon told her how much fun he'd had and that they should do it again; but Bonelwa never said a word until he stopped talking. When they arrived at her place, she said, "Thanks," and got out of the car.

"Hold up, let me walk you to your apartment."

"It's okay, Simon, there is no need. Bye."

"Bye," Simon replied and drove off.

CHAPTER TWENTY-TWO

onelwa decided to take a break from entertaining any dates and decided instead to focus on writing a memoir on her life thus far. She bought some books about learning how to write a book and studied them.

When she finished studying them, she began to write her memoir, but she soon realized that writing a book is easier in the head than it is to put it on paper. So she got stuck on the second page. However, she was determined to finish it, so she did an online search and found out that there was an authors' club in her area where authors help and encourage each other.

They met every week on Thursdays at six thirty in the evening, and it was open to anyone interested. She wrote down the address and put a reminder on her phone.

On Thursday, after work, she took a taxi and went to the authors' meeting. She was earlier than most of them, so she had to wait for the rest to arrive. When they were all set, the leader of the club opened the meeting, gave a few announcements, and asked if there was anyone that was there for the first time. Bonelwa and two other newcomers raised their hands. The group leader asked them to introduce themselves, which they did. When that was done, he proceeded with the agenda for that day, which was, "How to deal with writer's block." She sat there listening as different writers gave different kinds of advice on how each of them dealt with writer's block, and she took note. Then the leader asked if anyone had a finished chapter that they would like to read to the club and get feedback. Only one member raised his hand, an old Struggle Veteran, who read the third chapter of his second book, which was about his personal account of some incidents, in which he was personally involved, during the apartheid era.

The meeting ended at about eight o'clock, and Bonelwa stood on the other side of the road waiting for a taxi. A car pulled over, the driver lowered his window screen and said, "Bonelwa, right?"

"Yes…" she said, looking at him closer to see if she knew him from somewhere.

"It's Jack Cekete. We were together at the authors' club, I was one of the newcomers," he said.

"Oh… yes, Jack, I remember you."

"Where are you heading? I can give you a ride," he offered.

"I'm going to Rivonia."

"Okay, jump on in, I'm heading that way."

Bonelwa looked on both sides, unsure if it was safe to go with him.

"Okay, thank you," she said, got into the car and they drove off.

"So what are you busy writing at the moment?" Jack asked.

"I can barely call it writing; it's a memoir about my life, and I've only written one and a half pages," she replied.

"That's a great start! I've been staring at a blank page on my laptop for the past three months and can't quite seem to put the words onto paper. The funny thing is, I know in my mind what I want to say, but when I try to write it down, it doesn't quite come out the way I have it in my mind. What do you call that?"

"I don't know what it's called, but I think I have almost the same problem. What do you want to write about?"

"It's a "how to" book on marketing. It is aimed at sales people, to improve their marketing skills and increase sales... Yea, I know it is not as deep as a memoir."

"Not everything has to be deep; sometimes all we need is people, like you, to tell us what to do in plain language."

"Yea... I guess you're right about that."

"My take on books is that, if it fulfils the purpose it was written for, then it's a successful book, regardless of how many copies it sells or awards it gets. I guess we must just try to write our own books, rather than trying to write books similar to the books we've read. Otherwise, as long as we keep on comparing ourselves with the people whose books we've read, our writing will never be good enough for ourselves, let alone for others," Bonelwa said.

"Wow! You've just given me the answer I've been looking for all this time! Thanks," Jack said.

They continued to talk to each other, and by the time they arrived at Bonelwa's place, they had agreed to drive to the meetings and back together. Jack dropped Bonelwa off and went home.

Bonelwa and Jack continued to attend the writer's meetings together, while they both continued to craft their own books.

Six months passed, and slowly Bonelwa let down her guard, let Jack into her private space, and they started dating. Their relationship flourished with each moment they spent together. For the first time in a long time, Bonelwa felt loved, and was falling in love, with each day that she spent with Jack. She tried her best to keep their relationship outside the bedroom until she was completely sure that it was love and not lust on both parts. Jack was good-looking, intelligent and driven. And he talked a lot about building a better future, though not as a family, but about success and financial security.

On Bonelwa's twenty-eighth birthday, Jack suggested they celebrate it, just the two of them, at an upscale restaurant. Bonelwa was impressed with his initiative and was almost ready to declare it to be love. On Saturday night, he came to pick her up and they drove off to the upscale restaurant, which was a thirty-minute drive.

When they arrived there, they noticed that the place was more beautiful than what they had seen in the pictures. The waiter confirmed their reservation and led them to their reserved table. Jack pulled out the chair for Bonelwa and made sure that she was comfortable. "Thank you, Honey," she said with a secret smile and bright eyes.

"It is my pleasure, Luv," Jack said and went around to take a seat.

After perusing the menu they placed their orders.

"Thank you, Jack, this is a lovely place," she said.

"I'm glad you like it," he replied.

Jack stretched his hand across the table and held Bonelwa's hands and said, "Happy birthday, Luv."

"Thank you, Honey."

Their eyes locked as they held hands. After a little while, she turned her gaze back on him and said, "What do you really want from me, Jack?"

"I want to be with you," he said.

"But how? How do you want to be with me? Having fun or building a family?"

Jack looked down. The topic was making him uncomfortable. Continuing to look down he said, "I don't know, I mean, I don't know how it will all work out. Let's just take one step at the time."

"Okay," she said.

While the words were still in her mouth, the waiter brought their drinks. And as they continued to converse with each other, the waiter brought the food. Bonelwa asked the waiter to bring her a glass of water, with ice and lemon. He went to get it, returning in a dash with it, and left them to enjoy their meals. They talked and laughed while they ate and drank, and she smiled most of the time. She had not smiled like that since she broke up with Tau. The waiter came to clear the table when he noticed that they were done eating, and before he left, Jack gave him the secret signal go ahead. Jack had previously arranged with the waiter to bring a surprise birthday cake, when it was time. The waiter got the signal and went to fetch the cake.

When the waiter left their table, Jack's phone rang and he answered.

"Surprise! I'm home, please come fetch me at the airport," said the voice on the other side of the line.

"What do you mean you are home? What happened to Europe? I thought you were supposed to be there for more than one year."

"Yes, but I've changed my mind. Please come quickly."

"Okay, I will be right there."

"Who is that, Jack?" Bonelwa frowned.

"She… I… I have to go," he said looking down.

"It's my birthday, Jack," she shouted.

"She… She…"

"Who the hell is she, Jack? That she can call you on my birthday and you must jump and go?" she crossed her arms. And with her eyes wide open, she looked at him and demanded an answer.

"She is… she is my boss's daughter, and she is my fiancée… but she was supposed to be in London for a year."

"You bastard!" She grabbed her glass of water with ice and threw it at him, grabbed her bag and headed for the door. She met the waiter bringing her birthday cake, walked away and got into a cab. She sat in the back seat with tears pouring from her eyes all the way home.

When she got home, she was angry with herself for allowing herself to be fooled.

"Why? Why? What's wrong with me? I shut my heart, and I got good, sincere and loving men, who loved me with all their hearts… I open my heart and all I get is a bunch losers and cheaters," she said out loud to herself.

With violence, she took off the new outfit that she'd bought for her birthday and kicked off her high heels into her bedroom. Wearing her robe, she sat on the couch and turned on the TV, but paid no attention to it. Her mind was furiously hovering on Jack and how she could make him pay for taking her for a fool.

While busy planning her revenge, her favourite show came on TV. It took her mind off Jack and after the show, she decided he was not worthy of her time and energy, and instead she sat at her desk and wrote another chapter of her memoir. She felt better after writing.

She sat on the edge of her bed, preparing herself to sleep after putting on her night creams. "Never again, will I allow a man to treat me as Jack did," she thought to herself.

"No more dating for me, I'm done!" she said to herself, vowing to abstain from dating anyone, until she was absolutely sure that he was the one.

From that day on, Jack quit coming to the authors' meeting but she continued, glad that he had stopped coming.

She spent the next three years without dating and focused all her attention on mastering the art of writing.

On a winter Monday, her boss called her into her office and asked her to email some documents to their branch in Durban, and assigned her to a new post that dealt with communications with the Durban branch.

She left her boss's office and emailed the documents to Jabulani Dlamini, the head of communications of the Durban branch.

When Jabulani checked his emails that day, he opened Bonelwa's email and downloaded the document. While he read the document and the email, he noticed Bonelwa's email profile picture, enlarged it and said, "Brainy and pretty, that's a first."

Upon reading the document, he replied.

"Hi, Bonelwa, thank you for the documents."

"It is my pleasure, Sir. If you need anything else, just let me know, kind regards."

Bonelwa replied.

"Matter of fact I do; since you and I will be working very closely, it is only proper that we get to know each other. What about me buying you a cup of coffee on your lunch break Friday, after my meeting with the managing director there at head office?"

Jabulani replied.

Bonelwa looked left and right to make sure no one was looking and enlarged Jabulani's email profile picture, and thought, "Uhmm... you're very handsome, Jabulani... the question is... what do you really want?"

To make absolutely sure, she illegally pulled out his file from the system and checked his marital status—single. She then replied to Jabulani's request.

"Yes Sir, we can have coffee on Friday."

"Great, I'll see you on Friday then."

Jabulani replied.

"Okay, Sir, thank you."

She replied.

Friday, as agreed, Jabulani met with Bonelwa outside the Bank's office and the two went for coffee in the restaurant next to the bank.

At the restaurant they were seated by a grumpy waitress who was having a bad day. Bonelwa picked up her bad attitude, but decided not to entertain it. They placed their orders and sat opposite each other and avoided eye contact.

"So how long have you been working for the bank?" Jabulani tried to break the ice.

"Almost nine years." She replied.

"Wow! That's a long time."

"Yes, it is."

"Do you enjoy what you do?"

"Yes, I do."

"But?"

"But I love writing and talking. I hope one day I will able to do both and be able to support myself doing it."

"So you are a writer?"

"Yes, I am. Though not yet published, but who knows? Life is full of surprises."

"Yes, dreams do come true when we put our minds to it and work hard to accomplish them."

"Yes, I believe that too."

The waitress returned with their coffee and light lunch with a smile on her face; she hoped for a tip. They thanked her and continued with their conversation until they left the restaurant and went their separate ways.

On her way to the bank, she thought about Jabulani and the good time they'd had together. When she arrived at the office, with bright eyes and a smirk on her face, she caught Lerato's attention.

"What's gotten into you? You won the lottery, or what?" Lerato asked.

She smiled and replied, "I wish…" and went to her desk.

When she opened her emails, she found an email from Jabulani:

"Hey again, I really had a good time getting to know you today, we should do it again some other time."

"Yes, we should. I had a great time, too."

She replied.

"I'm leaving for Cape Town tomorrow, but I'll be back on Friday; what about dinner on Saturday night?"

"That would be nice."

"Okay, I'll see on Saturday then."

"Yes, thanks."

What was meant to be a working relationship, quickly drifted into a more personal than professional bond.

While Jabulani was in Cape Town, they exchanged numbers and talked almost every night that week.

Saturday, Jabulani picked her up and took her to an upscale restaurant. As they ate and conversed with each other, they opened up to each other and became relaxed in each other's company. Bonelwa found it hard to keep her vow and with each gaze at Jabulani, she opened the door of her heart an inch.

When they left the restaurant, she promised herself not to let him into her apartment just yet. Upon their arrival at Bonelwa's place, they sat in the car in the parking lot and talked with each other a bit more. She often gazed at him and wanted to be kissed by him, but restrained herself. After a while, she finally got the courage and said, "I better be going."

He rushed to get out of the car, opened the door for her, and walked her to her door. She opened her door and said, "Thanks." But he gave her no answer, his mind was preoccupied with whether he should kiss her or not.

She entered her apartment and turned around to look at him.

"Thanks for everything, I really had a lovely time tonight," she said as she held the door to close it.

"I'm glad you had a great time…" he said as their eyes locked.

They stood there without saying anything to each other. After a while, Jabulani prepared to leave and as he turned, she pulled him with both hands and kissed him with forceful passion. Then pushing him way with gentle delicacy and catching her breath, she said, "Bye." She closed the door and leaned against it with her eyes closed and a bright smile on her face.

Jabulani stared at the door and desperately wished she would once again open it and let him in. When he saw that was not on the table that night, he smiled at the door and left.

From that night things began to escalate, however, she didn't want their first sexual encounter to be an ordinary one, she wanted it to be special; therefore she kept him at bay when it came to sex.

Months passed and it was December. The bank booked a venue and rooms for all its employees at Beverly Hills Hotel, a five-star beach hotel in Umhlanga Rocks, in Durban, for their year-end party.

It was an evening to be remembered. The bank's CEO gave his keynote address and rewarded the best performing employees with different kinds of awards. Bonelwa was also asked to come forward to receive her award as the best performing employee at her branch. She didn't expect the award. She received the award, thanked all for it, and rushed to get out of the spotlight. When all that was done, the party officially began as the DJ played the greatest hits of the year. Bonelwa and Jabulani clung to each other and partied the whole night. It was after one in the morning when they called it a night and agreed to meet at Bonelwa's room; but to avoid office gossip, they left in turns. She left first and went to her room, ten minutes later he left and knocked at her door.

Bonelwa opened the door and hid behind it. He entered and stood at the centre of the room, and then heard a seductive voice behind him, "Hey, looking for something?"

"Yes, I'm looking for a very beautiful and sexy woman."

"You mean this one?" she said and dropped her gown. She was left wearing only new red lingerie. His eyes popped out seeing her gorgeous, well-toned body.

"Wow! Yes… this one," he said and approached her.

They spent the night consummating their passion, without restraining their desires, and giving their bodies no rest until their flesh had enough.

It was ten o'clock in the morning, when Bonelwa stretched out her arms to touch Jabulani, and realized that he was gone.

"Jabulani? … Honey?" But there was no answer.

She was too tired to get out of the bed to get her cell phone, so she decided to wait for him to return. She thought maybe he was having an early meeting with the executives, as he always had, for she knew that they never cease to work.

She fell asleep again and woke up at one o'clock in the afternoon, got out of bed, and that is when she saw the note from Jabulani, which read:

"Hi, it was fun, I hope this will do, thanks."

He left fifteen thousand rands with the note. Her eyes swelled with tears, her mind ran to and fro seeking an explanation for the ambiguous note and its significance to their relationship. Tears dropped from her eyes in fear that her assumption of the meaning of the letter could be true.

She tried not to panic. She wiped her tears, reached for her phone and called him. She was greeted by the most irritating voice…"The number you have dialled is not available at this moment."

She waited a bit and tried again, and got the same answer. She tried once again and got the same answer. She checked him on social media and found his update and a picture of him with his fiancée, which said, "One more week and I'm officially off the market!"

"What? It can't be! No, not again, it can't be!" she said as she looked out the hotel window. "How did I miss that?" she asked herself.

She sat on the edge of the bed and tears began to pour from her eyes as she asked herself, "Why? Why? Why can't I find someone that loves me and me alone? Why do I keep attracting men that just want to use me? What did I do to deserve this?"

In her desperate attempt to hide from the shame and the world, she closed all the curtains, laid on the bed, covered herself, including her head, and in darkness she poured out her tears without restraint. She fell asleep, crying.

The following morning when she woke up, she took a long shower, forcefully scrubbing herself, she wanted to cleanse any trace of Jabulani from her body. She got out of the shower, got dressed, and checked out of the hotel.

When she walked out the hotel's front door, and had moved a bit away, she took off her high heels, the heaviness in her heart made her high heels too hard to walk on.

"Come to Me, all you who labour and are heavy laden, and I will give you rest. Take My yoke upon you and learn from Me, for I am gentle and lowly in heart, and you will find rest for your souls. For My yoke is easy and My burden is light." (Matthew 11:28-30) The street preacher read out loud, as Bonelwa passed.

His voice sounded familiar to Bonelwa, so she turned to see the man who read out the Bible to those passing by, and she recognized him. It was the same street preacher that had told her, that God loved her. She stood there thinking whether it was coincidence that he was there, or something else. She stared at the preacher looking for answers. When the preacher saw her staring at him, he approached Bonelwa and said, "Miss, you can't get what you're seeking on your own, nor can you get it from anyone else. Only Jesus can give rest to your restless soul and peace to your troubled heart. All you have to do is accept Jesus' invitation and come to Him. How long will you continue to seek love and peace from people that end up disappointing you? Come to Jesus and you'll experience real love and peace of heart."

Bonelwa saw her bus coming and rushed to the bus station.

She rested at the bus station, waiting for the bus. The bus arrived and Solly was driving the bus.

"Hi, Solly," Bonelwa greeted him and showed him her ticket.

"Hi, Nelwa," Solly greeted her back.

"Are you okay?" Solly asked.

"Not really, but I will be," she replied.

She sat there and looked out the window with her eyes, but her bleeding heart was fixed on Jabulani. Solly looked at her in the rear view mirror, from time to time.

Six streets away from her stop, as the bus crossed the traffic lights, a speeding Ford SUV, chased by the police, suddenly crossed the red traffic lights and hit the bus on the driver's side, causing the bus to spin and overturn. The police that chased the robbers arrived at the scene and surrounded the SUV with their guns drawn and aimed at the robbers. When the police saw that the two robbers sitting in front bled heavily and were unconscious, they pulled them out of the car. The two robbers at the back came out of the car with their hands up and were arrested and handcuffed.

The paramedics and fire fighters arrived a few moments later, and quickly removed Solly, Bonelwa and the other twenty passengers from the bus to receive medical attention. When the paramedics attended to all involved in the accident, the two robbers that were pulled out from the front seats of the SUV were pronounced dead at the scene. Out of the twenty-two people that were on the bus, four were also pronounced dead at the scene, ten were severely wounded and rushed to a nearby hospital, while the rest only incurred minor injuries.

Bonelwa was one of the ten people severely injured and rushed to the hospital.

CHAPTER TWENTY-THREE

hree days later Bonelwa woke up in a hospital bed with a bandage over her head and left eye. She wanted to move her right hand but she couldn't, because she had a cast over her right shoulder and arm, she'd also fractured her left leg and had a cast over it.

She had tubes connected to her mouth and nostrils. She lifted up her left hand and her finger pulled away from the pulse machine, triggering the alarm, and causing the nurse assigned to her to rush and come check on her.

The nurse found her awake, and removed the tubes from her mouth.

"Ms. Hlazo, can you hear me?" the nurse asked.

"Yes… where am I?" Bonelwa asked.

"You're in the hospital. You were involved in a very terrible car accident, it's a miracle you're alive."

She looked around and tried to remember what had happened but she couldn't.

"Dr. Ntuli will be here in about an hour to check on you," the nurse said.

"Okay," she replied.

"He'll be able to give you more details about your condition."

"Okay."

"Don't worry, you're in very good hands. Dr. Ntuli is an excellent doctor, and a beautiful soul with the hands of an angel. You should thank him, he saved your life."

"I will."

"And I don't mean just by treating you," the nurse continued. "When we couldn't find your medical aid card, you were about to be transferred to a public hospital. But he fought against the decision and offered to pay your medical bills if you didn't have medical aid. He signed to take full responsibility for your hospitalization."

"Thank you for letting me know… I'll make sure to thank him."

"Okay, please rest now. I'll wake you up when the doctor is here."

"Okay, thank you."

An hour later the doctor arrived at Bonelwa's ward.

"Ms. Hlazo… Ms. Hlazo…" the nurse woke her up.

"Umm… uhmm… yes," she woke up.

"The doctor is here."

"Okay… thank you."

The nurse left the ward while the doctor pulled up a chair to sit next to her.

"How are you feeling Ms. Hlazo?"

"I don't know… my head is heavy and my body is numb."

"That's normal for people in your condition."

"Okay."

"Do you remember anything?"

"No, I have this blank in my memory."

"It is caused by the impact you suffered to your head, but sooner or later things will start coming back to you."

"Okay."

"Ms. Hlazo, you were involved in a serious collision between the bus you were riding on and a SUV. You were injured on the head and left eye; you fractured your right shoulder and arm and your left leg."

"Will I be able to use my arm and run again?"

"Yes, with the help of a physiotherapist, you may fully recover. But for now, let's focus on getting you well and getting you out of this bed."

"Thank you, Dr. Ntuli, for everything you've done for me. Thank you for saving my life," she said with tears rolling down her face.

"Please don't mention it, I was just doing my job."

"No Doctor, you went way beyond the line of duty. I was told about the sacrifice you made for me, thank you…" tears poured from her eyes, "I will pay you back as soon as I can, I promise."

"Please don't worry about it. I want you to focus on getting better."

"Okay… but I'll pay you back, I promise."

"Let's talk about that after you get out of this bed and can remember things."

"Okay, thank you."

After some further instructions, the doctor left.

The following day when Bonelwa woke, she found the morning shift nurse kneeling down next to her bed praying, her hands stretched over Bonelwa's body. Bonelwa watched the nurse as she softly prayed for her. Bonelwa decided to close her eyes. She wanted to pray also, but she didn't know what to say, so she decided to wait until the nurse finished praying. The nurse got up when she was done praying and headed for the door.

"Thank you for praying for me," Bonelwa said in her sickly voice, as the nurse was about to get out of the room.

"Ms. Hlazo... I'm sorry... I didn't know you were awake..." the nurse replied.

"No need to apologize... I surely need all your prayers," Bonelwa said.

"My name is Anne, I will be looking after you throughout the day shift," the nurse introduced herself to Bonelwa.

"Okay... thank you... if you don't mind me asking, what exactly were you praying for me?" Bonelwa asked.

Anne smiled and replied, "I don't mind... I was asking God to completely heal your body... and if you're not saved, that He may grant you grace to repent and save your soul."

"Okay... thank you... how do I get saved?" Bonelwa asked with a serious tone in her voice.

"I'm not much of a preacher... but I know, if you want to be saved, you must repent of all your sins, have a change of heart toward God, and that is made possible by you believing that Jesus died for your sins on the cross. You must ask God to forgive you for all your sins, in the name of Jesus, and you must put your trust in God's love and mercy by putting your trust in Jesus Christ... I don't know if I'm making any sense to you... I can go get someone better qualified that would explain better how salvation works...would you like me to go get someone?" Anne explained.

"No Anne... there is no need, I get it... I think I understand what you mean," Bonelwa replied.

"Do you mind if I read you a few verses from the Bible that would better explain what I've just rambled about?" Anne asked.

"No... I would love to hear it... please go right ahead," Bonelwa replied.

Anne took a Bible from the drawer next to Bonelwa's bed and opened the Bible to Romans chapter ten, and read verses six through thirteen:

"But the righteousness of faith speaks in this way, 'Do not say in your heart, "'Who will ascend into heaven?'" (that is, to bring Christ down *from above*) or, "'Who will descend into the abyss?'" (that is, to bring Christ up from the dead). But what does it say? "The word is near you, in your mouth and in your heart" (that is, the word of faith which we preach): that if you confess with your mouth the Lord Jesus and believe in your heart that God has raised Him from the dead, you will be saved. For with the heart one believes unto righteousness, and with the mouth confession is made unto salvation. For the Scripture says, "Whoever believes on Him will not be put to shame." For there is no distinction between Jew and Greek, for the same Lord over all is rich to all who call upon Him. For "whoever calls on the name of the Lord shall be saved."

After reading, Anne looked at Bonelwa and said, "The way I understand it, is that you can be saved anywhere, and in any circumstance, all you need is your mouth and your heart; your mouth to confess Jesus as your Lord and Saviour, and your heart to believe that Jesus Christ died for your sins and that God raised Him from the dead for your justification. According to the Bible, if you call upon God and ask for forgiveness in the name of Jesus Christ, you will be saved," Anne explained.

"Sounds so simple... yet it's not that easy," Bonelwa said.

"Would you like us to pray together?" Anne asked.

"No… Thanks anyway, Anne. The truth is, I'm not ready… there are three people that I deeply hate, and I don't think I can ask God to forgive me, if I am not ready to forgive them… but I will call upon God," Bonelwa replied.

"Okay… I understand… just remember, you can come to God just as you are at any time while the door of salvation is still open," Anne cautioned Bonelwa.

"Okay… thank you, Anne," Bonelwa said.

"Please rest, the doctor will come by a little later to check up on you," Anne said.

"Okay, Anne, thank you for everything."

Anne left to check on her other patients and Bonelwa went back to sleep.

Later that day the doctor came by at around the same time as the previous day, and found Bonelwa awake.

"How is my favourite patient in the whole world?" the doctor asked.

"I feel better than yesterday, thank you," Bonelwa replied

"Do you remember anything?"

"No… nothing at all… only that I deeply hate three people."

"Please give it time, it will all eventually come back to you."

"I hope so."

Days passed and the doctor continued to check up on her daily.

On the eighth day, the doctor found her, bed reclined, watching TV.

"Well, well… this is a surprise!" said the doctor. "By the looks of it, you're recovering well."

"Yes, Doctor, I feel much better, thank you… and the best part is that, I can remember almost everything."

"That's great news!"

"Yes, it is; I work for a bank and I do have medical aid. The reason I didn't have it with me that day, is because I was coming back from a party the bank had organized for its employees."

"Okay, I'm just glad that you've regained your memory."

"Yes, to be honest, I was panicking. I'd have to live the rest of my life without knowing about my past… and even though now that I remember almost everything, and I wish some of the things would've remained in the land of forgetfulness… I'm still glad to have my memory back."

"Yes… that's a good thing… and how is your head?"

"It's starting to feel light."

"And how is your right shoulder and arm?"

"The pain has minimized… it's just itchy sometimes and I can't scratch myself."

"Okay… and your left leg, can you feel it?

"Yes, I can!"

"Okay, unless there are any unforeseen complications, you will be able to go home in a few days."

"Really?"

"Yes."

"Thank you, Doctor!"

He left her ward and went to attend to his other patients. Five days later he came to see her at the usual time.

"I have good news for you, Ms. Hlazo, you're out of here!" the doctor discharged her.

"Thank you, Doctor! I can't wait to get home."

"Just one thing… if you want to be able to run again, you'll have to put a lot of effort in to fully recover."

"I will."

"Listen, I took the liberty to speak with a friend of mine, who is a physiotherapist, and she has agreed to work with you. Please don't worry about the cost, I've already taken care of it; all you have to do is to say yes."

"Yes, I'll work with her, but I'll pay you all back, as soon I can."

"No problem."

"Thank you again for everything, Doctor, I really appreciate all that you've done for me."

"It's my pleasure, Nelwa."

The room went quiet after he called her "Nelwa", and after an intense silence she asked, "How do you know me as Nelwa? Only very few people know me as Nelwa and I know all of them… and you are not one of them. What's going on, Doctor?"

"You really don't remember me, do you?"

"No, I don't," she said, looking at him and trying to remember if she knew him.

"Maybe it's the beard and the glasses," he said, and removed his glasses.

"I still don't remember you."

"It's Senzo, from University of Cape Town… the one you dumped."

Bonelwa became quiet and looked at him in disbelief, as his face suddenly became familiar.

"Oh Senzo! Yes, I remember you… that was ten years ago."

"Yes."

"I'm so sorry, Senzo… you know… for dumping you like that."

"Don't worry about it, it was a long time ago."

"Wow! Look at you… A doctor! I'm very proud of you."

"Thank you."

The conversation was interrupted by Anne with a wheelchair to take Bonelwa to the parking lot.

"Is someone picking you up?" Senzo asked. He and Anne helped Bonelwa get in the wheelchair.

"No, I'll get a cab," Bonelwa replied.

"A cab? No way! I'll give you a ride and I'm not taking a no for an answer," Senzo said.

Anne reached for her handbag, took out a gift, and handed it over to Bonelwa saying, "This is for you."

"Thank you, Anne… thank you," Bonelwa said. And then asked, "What is it?"

"It is for you to find out," Anne said and smiled.

Senzo told Anne not worry, he'll push Bonelwa's wheelchair to the parking lot. Bonelwa and Senzo headed to reception, picked up her belongings, and went to the parking lot.

After helping Bonelwa into the car, they heard a voice calling, "Ms. Hlazo… Ms. Hlazo."

They both looked in the direction from where the voice was coming and saw a police officer coming toward them.

"Ms. Hlazo, I'm Officer David Moabelo. I was asked by the chief investigator of this case to hand you this letter in person, it was found in one of the pockets of the late Solly Maloka, the bus driver. It is addressed to you," the officer said.

"Oh my God, is Solly dead?" she asked in tears.

"Yes Ma'am, I'm afraid so. I'm so sorry for your loss," he handed her the letter.

"Thank you," she said, wiping the tears pouring from her eyes.

They drove off while the officer watched, and a few minutes later arrived at her place. Senzo helped her into her apartment and went back to work.

Bonelwa sat on the couch, opened and read Solly's letter:

"Dear Nelwa,

The first time I laid my eyes on you, my heart was stricken with awe at your beauty. You are the most beautiful woman I have ever seen. Your authentic personality is the invisible sparkle that makes you a very beautiful soul, inside and out.

"I've been driving you on the bus for years, yet each time I attempted to tell you how I feel about you, the scars in your heart, made visible by the sadness in your eyes, would not let me. So, I decided to write you this letter. I'm in love with you, Nelwa. I hope one day my love can take the sadness away from your heart and bring a bright smile to your beautiful face.

I love you,
Solly"

"Oh Solly… I love you too! You were the most caring soul I've ever met," Bonelwa burst into tears.

That day, Senzo left the hospital with his mind on ten years ago. Seeing Bonelwa again, set his suppressed feelings for her afire all over again. He was madly in love with her at university.

That day when he got home, he went straight to his study room and tried to write.

Senzo was thirty-one years old, a year younger than Bonelwa. He was good-looking, fit and well-mannered. He had brown eyes and broad shoulders.

He came from a very affluent family in Kwazulu-Natal; his grand-father was once the mayor of eThekwini - Durban.

He was a bookworm since he began to read, and always dreamed of becoming a writer one day. But his parents had discouraged him, advising him to pursue a "real career" and take writing as a hobby, and he'd heeded them.

He graduated from high school without a high school sweet-heart, his love for reading alienated him from interested girls. He just couldn't find a girl that loved reading as much as he did.

It was his freshman year when he'd met Bonelwa and found in her all that he ever wanted in a girl. However, Bonelwa's heart was already taken and broken; the eyes of her heart were blinded by pain. So, she used him and broke his heart.

That day when he saw Bonelwa lying unconscious and helpless on a hospital bed, reminded him of how she broke his heart and how much he still loved her. After attending to her and getting her stabilized, he looked at her ring finger and was relieved to see no wedding ring.

He sat in his study room, staring at a blank page on his laptop, not knowing what to write.

~* ~* ~* ~

Bonelwa sat on the edge of her bed and unwrapped the gift Anne gave her, it was an expensive leather bound Bible. "Why am I not surprised?" Bonelwa said to herself, and placed the Bible on her left side lampstand.

CHAPTER TWENTY-FOUR

A few days later, Senzo brought the physiotherapist by and introduced her to Bonelwa, and the two began to work on Bonelwa's rehabilitation. Senzo also helped as much as he could. On weekends, he would help Bonelwa with some household errands and take her to the mall to do her shopping.

As her therapy progressed, she began to walk with a crutch and was able to use her right arm.

A week later, she wanted to return to work but her manager told her to finish her therapy first and wait until she had fully recovered, and she agreed. However, spending most of her time indoors began to frustrate her and she became depressed.

When Senzo came to check on her one day, he found her moody and wallowing in self-pity, so he decided to take her to the park, near her apartment.

At the park, after finding a free bench in the shade, each took out their books and began to read, as was their custom. A few minutes later, Bonelwa closed her book and looked at Senzo. While Senzo continued to read, he felt as if someone was staring at him; he took his eyes away from the book and scanned through the park until his eyes met the piercing eyes of Bonelwa, staring at him.

"What?" he asked.

"Nothing," she replied.

"Are you okay?" Senzo asked.

"No, I'm not, Senzo. I just can't stop thinking about the horrible things I've done to you."

"It's okay, Nelwa, it was a long time ago."

"No, Senzo, it's not okay… I'm really sorry for hurting you… please forgive me."

"I've forgiven you a long time ago; but it's you that must forgive yourself."

"How, Senzo? How?"

"By accepting that you've made a mistake and that you cannot change the past. No amount of guilt will undo the past; you must just let the past go, embrace the present, and hope for the future."

"Okay, I hear you… and thank you for forgiving me."

"I was hurt then, but I'm over it now; besides, we were both very young and foolish, though my love for you was real and mature."

"Yes, I remember… you were so serious and sincere about your love for me that it touched me… but I was too deeply hurt to care and appreciate it."

Senzo looked into her eyes, held her hand and said, "I'm just glad to be here and enjoying this moment with you. Let's not ruin it by dwelling on the past, since none of us can change what happened there. I'm very much happy with now and filled with hope for to-morrow."

"You're right, me too."

They went back to their reading until the sun was setting. They left the park and Senzo got some Chinese take-away on their way back to her apartment.

They sat on her couch and ate while they conversed with each other about the characters of the books they were reading. Their sweet conversation was interrupted, when Senzo's phone rang. He picked it up and ended the phone conversation by saying, "I'll be right there."

Then he turned to Bonelwa and said, "I've got to attend to a personal matter, I'll see you tomorrow after work."

"Okay," she replied.

Her sad eyes followed Senzo as he left her apartment; her mind could not help but to assume that the person that called was his significant other. The following day Senzo called after work to let her know that he was on his way to check up on her, but she didn't pick up his calls.

After three days of trying to reach her without any success; he decided to stop by her apartment. He knocked at her door.

"It's open, please come on in!" She shouted. She thought it was the pizza delivery guy with the pizza she had ordered moments ago.

"Oh, it's you," she said when she saw that it was Senzo.

"Yes, it's me," he replied. "Why are you not picking up my calls? Have I done something wrong?"

"Senzo, it's clear you have someone in your life, so let's not complicate our lives. I don't have time, nor energy, for this thing...or whatever your game plan is."

"Thing? Game plan? What are you talking about?"

"I'm talking about whoever summoned you the other day and you rushed off to her."

"Oh, I see; is that what this is all about?"

"Senzo, you have someone in your life, just admit it."

"Yes, I do… and I never said that I didn't."

"Why are you here then, Senzo? For this is way beyond your doctor's duty."

"I'm here because I care about you… I never really stopped loving you… I just learned to live without you."

"Senzo… please… let's not go there."

"Go where? That I love you?"

"Senzo… please…"

"Nelwa, you have to stop running away from my love."

"I'm not running away this time, Senzo… you have someone in your life."

"Yes, I do, but she's no obstacle to my love for you, unless you make her to be."

"Senzo… please… what do you want from me?"

"Nothing more than you're prepared to give."

"What do you want me to do? What am I supposed to do when you have someone else in your life?"

"Wait until you meet her and then decide."

"Why would I want to do that?"

"I've spoken to her and she's okay with it."

"I'm not."

"I've to go before she calls me again. We'll come by on the weekend, bye!"

He said and rushed out the door.

Her sad eyes once again followed Senzo, as he walked out of her apartment. Her mind could not help but conclude that the person that he was rushing to see was his better half.

She forcefully turned off the TV and angrily grabbed her crutches wanting to go to bed. While she walked, she groused and murmured, not paying much attention to where she was going, and suddenly she tripped and fell to the ground. She felt an excruciating pain in her broken leg, but compared to the pain in her heart, it felt mild. With her face turned to the floor, tears started to pour out. The burden of her heart made her unwilling to get up. "I surrender… I surrender…" she cried out loud, tears of pain pouring from her eyes. "I can't carry on like this… this pain and hatred has eaten me up… I don't know who I am anymore… Jesus… if You are really there… please save me… please forgive me all my sins… there are too many… please forgive me for hating Tau, Zuki and Eric… I forgive them all… I forgive them… I surrender my hatred and desire to avenge myself for all that they did to me… please take away my hurt, pain and sorrow and set me free… I want to be free… please save me oh Lord… save me… I'm yours… Jesus… I surrender my life to you… wash me in your blood and please give me a new heart… I don't want this one anymore… I don't want to hate anyone… please save me in the name of Jesus… Amen."

While still stretched on the floor, she continued to plead with God to save her soul. And while she was busy repenting and confessing her sins before God, God took away her guilt, gave her a new heart, and put His joy in her heart.

"Thank you, Lord… for forgiving me and taking my guilt away… thank you for filling my heart with joy… I'm yours now… please help me to live for You from now on." She thanked God and raised herself up. The Bonelwa that fell to the ground died on the ground, the one that got up, was a new Bonelwa.

~* ~* ~* ~

On Saturday, at around eleven o'clock in the morning, they knocked on Bonelwa's door. Bonelwa limped to get the door without her crutches.

"Hi," Senzo greeted.

"Hi," Bonelwa greeted back.

"Bonelwa, meet Lwazi; Lwazi, meet Bonelwa, the friend I've spoken to you about," Senzo introduced them to each other.

"Hi, Lwazi, nice meeting you," Bonelwa greeted Lwazi.

"The pleasure is all mine; I've heard a lot of good things about you," Lwazi stretched out her hand to shake Nelwa's.

"Nelwa, meet the only woman in my life, my six year old daughter, Lwazi," Senzo announced.

"Come on in," Bonelwa invited them in.

Bonelwa served them some drinks and muffins and sat with them on the sofa. She signalled Senzo, with her teeth locked, "I'm going to kill you!"

Senzo laughed at her threat, and said, "Lwazi loves ice-skating, and I promised to take her today, would you care to join us?"

"No, I don't think it's a good idea for me to go ice-skating with my broken leg."

"Lwazi will be ice-skating, we'll be watching. Come on, it's going to be fun," Senzo persisted.

"Yes. It'll be fun, I promise," Lwazi ganged up with father in convincing Nelwa.

After thinking for a while, she said, "Okay, let me just change and we'll go."

"Yeah!" Lwazi and her dad shouted.

Bonelwa came out of her bedroom, all dressed up, and the three went ice-skating. When they arrived, Senzo bought the ticket and after putting on her ice-skates, Lwazi entered the rink and spread her hands like wings as she ice-skated.

Senzo and Bonelwa sat on the bench and watched Lwazi ice-skating and waving at them each time she passed by them.

"She's beautiful, Senzo!" Bonelwa said.

"Yeah, thanks! She looks like her mother."

"Where is her mother?"

"She passed away two years back."

"Oh, I'm so sorry, Senzo."

"Thanks, it was hard for us in the beginning, but we are fine now."

"What happened?"

"She had breast cancer."

"I'm so sorry to hear that, Senzo… how is Lwazi coping with all of this?"

"She is stronger than I am. She gives me strength when I'm down and miss her mother."

Bonelwa emotionally shook her head in agreement.

"What I miss the most about Khanyi, is her protective ways. She once saved my life and protected me thereafter.

After you dumped me, I was deeply hurt and gave up on love. I started hanging out with the wrong crowd and broke the hearts of some very good girls that loved and cared for me. Things got worse when I started abusing alcohol and, later on, drugs.

After I've got my degree, I came here for my practical. One day, I left a bar not far from here, so drunk that I could barely walk. I was attacked by some robbers, who cleaned up whatever I had left in my pockets and left me bleeding on the pavement. And that is where Khanyi found me. She was coming from church with her brother when she saw me, and she and her brother carried me to the car, took me to their home, prayed for me, bound my wounds, and let me stay with them. In the morning, when I woke up, the first face I saw was hers. She had a face that radiated with love and hands that felt like balm. She introduced herself to me and told me what had happened. She was wearing a nurse's uniform and was on her way to work night shift at a nearby hospital, but she wanted to feed me first, before going to work. After feeding me, she left for work.

I spent seven days in their house, without drinking or taking drugs. On the eighth day she invited me to go to church with them, I complied mostly out of duty. But at church, after the pastor preached, he asked for people to come forward and I found myself joining with those who were going. We were told to lay down whatever burden was weighing us down and ask the Lord to take it. I knelt and prayed there. I don't know... I'm not worthy to be a Christian, but I left that house a different man, and I have not been the same person ever since.

I quickly realized that spending time with her kept me out of trouble, so I started hanging out with her as much as I could. A year later, we got married and five years later I lost her to cancer. But before she left, she gave me this precious gift, so that when I miss her, I can always look at Lwazi and see Khanyi in her eyes," Senzo told Bonelwa.

Bonelwa sat there, looking at Senzo, with a guilty conscience and sympathy at the same time. She didn't know what to say, so she leaned on his shoulder.

Lwazi got tired and came out of the ice-rink. They went to grab something to eat and went back to Bonelwa's place, dropped her off, and Senzo and Lwazi went home.

Senzo and Bonelwa continued to see each other and occasionally spent time together with Lwazi. The more time they spent together, the more they both realized just how perfect they were for each other.

Almost five months after the accident, Bonelwa notified her boss that she was ready to return to work. However, her boss had some bad news for her. With the recession looming that year, the bank decided to cut costs and shut down her department and retrench all employees in her department, including her boss. Bonelwa was devastated at the news that she'd lost her job.

When Senzo came by that day, she told him the bad news.

"I'm so sorry to hear that," Senzo tried to comfort her.

"I don't know what I'm going to do. Getting another job in this recession will be a mission," Bonelwa despaired.

"Wait a minute... why don't you go back to university and finish your degree? I'll pay for it, and you can do what you always dreamed of."

"I'm not sure, Senzo, it's been so long since I last attended a class, I don't know if I can still do it."

"Of course you can! You're one of the brightest women I've ever met. You'll be out of there in no time."

"I think you're right, Senzo."

"Of course, I am."

"I can't believe I threw my dream away, because of a heartbreak."

"Don't beat yourself about it, you were young and foolish, like I was. Take this as a second chance to reach your dream."

"Yes, I will. Thank you, Senzo. Let me get my laptop and enrol myself in the next open course."

"That's the spirit!"

She got up and grabbed her laptop and, together, they enrolled her at the University of Johannesburg.

A few months later, she began to attend classes. She was overwhelmed by the demands of studying fulltime and she wanted to quit, but Senzo encouraged her to stay on and finish it.

After a year and few months, she completed her degree. Senzo and Lwazi attended her graduation ceremony and took her out to celebrate.

As they sat there, eating and drinking as they celebrated, Bonelwa looked at Senzo and Lwazi as they shared their food and played with each other. Her mind took her back to when she was twenty years old, it was the picture she had envisioned of her life back then, and tears started flowing from her eyes.

"Are you okay?" Lwazi asked, noticing her tears.

"Yes, Honey, I'm fine," Bonelwa replied and quickly wiped her tears.

"Hey... what's wrong?" Senzo asked.

"I'm fine... I guess I'm just a little overwhelmed... I'm so happy to have you both in my life... but I'm afraid that I might lose you... nothing in my life ever lasts."

"Why would you think that? We are not going anywhere," Lwazi said.

Senzo stretched his arm across the table, held Bonelwa's hand and said,

"Hey… look at me… this one will last, we are going nowhere."

"Okay… okay," Bonelwa wiped her tears.

After celebrating, they went on their way, dropped Bonelwa off, and Senzo and Lwazi went home.

CHAPTER TWENTY-FIVE

onelwa spent the next month job hunting without any success. She felt more and more depressed with each jobless day that passed.

When her thirty third birthday came, she was in no celebratory mood. However, Lwazi and Senzo insisted that they go out and celebrate. When she saw that there was no way for her to escape, she agreed, and they went out.

Senzo and Lwazi planned everything with the restaurant. When they arrived, the waiter led them to their reserved table and seated them, then departed to get their drinks. He came back with a bottle of non-alcoholic champagne and cold drink for Lwazi.

"May I pour you a glass of champagne, Ma'am?" the waiter asked.

"Yes, please," Bonelwa accepted.

After he poured Bonelwa and Senzo a glass of champagne, and help Lwazi with her can of cold drink, he asked them for their orders; after taking their orders, he left.

Bonelwa took a sip of the champagne and said, "Thank you both, this is a very lovely and fancy place to celebrate my birthday."

"You're welcome," Lwazi said.

Senzo raised his glass and said, "Happy birthday, Honey, may you have many more."

"Thank you, Honey, for not letting me wallow in self-pity, I would've missed this beautiful evening with the two of you!"

"Honey, don't get ahead of yourself, the evening, is still young," Senzo said.

"What do you mean?" Bonelwa asked.

The conversation was interrupted by the waiter with their special meals.

"Thank you," they all thanked the waiter.

"Lwazi, please pray for us," Senzo requested.

"Okay, Dad… let's close our eyes," she requested. "Dear God, please bless our food and make this night a very special night, in Jesus' name I pray, Amen!"

"Amen!" Senzo and Bonelwa replied.

As they feasted and conversed with each other, they made each other laugh, as each one told their funny stories. When they were done with their meals, the waiter came to clear the table. And as arranged by Senzo, fifteen minutes later, the waiter came with his fellow waiters carrying a big cake with thirty-three lit candles. He put the cake on the table and they all sang happy birthday to her. Bonelwa could not hold back her tears of joy as she blew out the candles. Then the waiters left their table, leaving the three of them alone.

"Happy birthday! Here, this is for you," Lwazi handed Bonelwa her present.

"Thank you, Lwazi! What is it?" Bonelwa asked.

"Open up and see," Lwazi replied.

Bonelwa quickly opened the present, "Oh, it's a beautiful photo frame, thank you, Honey!"

"No, it's not a photo frame," Lwazi protested.

"Is not?" Bonelwa asked, "What is it, Sweetheart?"

"It's a wedding photo frame. It's for you to put in your most beautiful wedding photo," Lwazi explained.

"Oh yes, now I see, you're right. I'll make sure I do just that, thank you, Lwazi!"

"You're welcome."

Then they both turned their gaze on Senzo and he stared right back at them. Lwazi motioned Senzo to give Bonelwa his present.

Senzo got up from his chair, knelt down and took a small gift box from his pocket, and said, "Happy birthday, Sweetheart... Bonelwa Hlazo, will you marry me?"

"Oh... Senzo..." Bonelwa covered her mouth with both hands.

Lwazi gazed at her, expectantly. Bonelwa turned and looked at Lwazi looking for approval, Lwazi nodded her head in agreement and whispered, "Say yes."

Bonelwa looked straight into Senzo's eyes, it was the same look he gave her almost twelve years ago. She took the box from his hand and said, "Yes! I will marry you!"

She unwrapped the box and opened it, inside was a seven carat diamond ring. She gave the box back to Senzo who was still on his knee, and said, "Will you do me the honour?"

"With pleasure," Senzo took the ring and placed it on Bonelwa's finger, and they kissed and hugged each other. Lwazi covered her mouth with her right hand and laughed when they kissed.

Bonelwa and Senzo hugged each other tight, they didn't want to let go.

"I will not let you go this time!" Senzo said with tears dropping from his eyes, and squeezed her even tighter to himself.

"I'll never again take your love for granted," Bonelwa said into his ear with tearful eyes.

Lwazi went around the table and hugged them with her tiny hands. Bonelwa and Senzo embraced her.

"Does this mean, I can now call you Mummy?" Lwazi asked.

"Yes, Sweetheart... you can call me Mummy... I'd love that!" Bonelwa could no longer contain her tears.

A few moments later, they all took their seats, and Senzo poured another glass of champagne for Bonelwa and himself, refilled Lwazi's glass with cold drink, and said, "I would like to propose a toast, please raise your glasses."

They all raised their glasses.

"May this moment of happiness never depart from our lives; may we remain together, as a family, in good and bad times, and may we forever love and accept each other." They clinked the glasses to seal the toast.

As the evening progressed, Lwazi fell asleep on Bonelwa's lap. But the two love birds continued to have their seemingly never-ending sweet conversation. However, at one o'clock in the morning, they decided to call it a night. Senzo asked the waiter to pack the cake in a take-away box and bring the bill. He settled it, generously tipped the waiter for the excellent service, and they departed.

The following week, Senzo took Bonelwa to his parents' home in Durban for the weekend. Bonelwa was nervous to meet his parents. She feared that they might not approve of her, since they were upper class society people. But her fears were put to rest when Senzo's mother welcomed her with a genuinely warm smile and open arms.

Senzo's mother's heart warmed up to her even more, when she heard Lwazi calling Bonelwa, Mummy.

After discussing the wedding arrangements with Senzo's mother, who promised that she would take care of everything, they returned to Johannesburg with a set wedding date.

On Sunday, as was his custom, Senzo took Lwazi and Bonelwa to church. After church, he briefed the pastor about the wedding plans. The pastor was happy for him and Lwazi. Senzo invited the pastor and his wife for lunch the following Sunday after church, to properly introduce Bonelwa to them, and the pastor agreed.

The next Sunday, after church, Senzo, Bonelwa and Lwazi arrived home with the pastor and his wife. Bonelwa had cooked and baked for them before they left for church. After lunch, they sat in the lounge and the pastor gave them some counselling, and told them that he was available for further counselling, if they wanted. They both thanked the pastor and his wife and escorted them out as they were leaving.

The wedding date was fast approaching, and Bonelwa was worried that she had no one to give her away on her wedding day. Since she had broken the family tradition of keeping her virginity until marriage, she didn't want to involve her family, in order to spare them of the gossip.

She sat at the edge of her bed in her apartment, thinking about who could give her away. After ruling out a few possibilities, she remember of Dr. Vusi Ndalo, whom she'd met in the park once, and had told her that if she ever needed anything, she should not hesitate to contact him. She decided to give it a shot, so she went to look for his business card, found it, and called him right away.

"Hello," the old man answered.

"Hello, Dr. Ndalo. My name is Bonelwa, I don't know if you still remember me, but I once met you in central park and you gave me your card. You told me if I ever needed anything, I should not hesitate to call you, well, I need a favour from you."

"Okay, I'm listening."

"I would like to talk to you."

"You're not going ask me on the phone, if you can call me, are you?"

"No Sir... I see you do remember me."

"Of course I do, Bonelwa. What can I do for you?"

"Can I buy you a cup of coffee?"

"Is that a bribe?"

"No Sir..."

"Okay... I know just the place, where they sell very expensive coffee... Candid Café, I always wanted to go there, but they're ridiculously expensive! But, since you'll be buying, I would gladly meet you there. What do you say?"

"No problem, Dr. Ndalo, it's fine by me."

"Okay, then let's meet there on Friday morning at eleven o'clock sharp. If you are one minute late, the appointment will be cancelled; even if we meet at the door, on my way out, I'll pretend I don't know you. Do you understand me?"

"Yes, Sir, I do...thank you."

"Okay, then, I'll see you there on Friday. Thank you for calling, bye," the old man said and hung up.

Friday morning, at half past ten, Bonelwa was at Candid Café, where they agreed to meet. At quarter to eleven, Dr. Ndalo showed up and sat opposite Bonelwa.

"Because you've agreed to my terms, and you can take instruction, I will pay for the coffee and do whatever I can to help you with whatever you need. Now, let me give you a warning, if you try false humility with me and think that you're being polite by saying that you don't mind paying, I will let you pay!" said the doctor.

"Okay, Dr. Ndalo… thank you for coming," Bonelwa replied.

Bonelwa told him about her reason for meeting him and was as candid as she could be with him about everything. She ended by saying, "So I need someone to give me away to the man who loves me more than I love myself, would you do me the honour?"

"You're a very brave young woman, I love that! Strong and bold! I would gladly be your father that day," Dr. Ndalo said.

"Thank you, Dr. Ndalo… thank you!"

"It would be my pleasure… however, I've a proposition for you…"

"Okay… I'm all ears."

"Try to reach out to your parents. Make peace with them and give your father a chance to walk you down the aisle…if he refuses, I'll gladly walk you down the aisle."

Bonelwa went quiet, in deep thought.

"Bonelwa, I know this is difficult for you, but please give it a try, okay?"

Bonelwa nodded her head in agreement, sighed deeply and said, "Okay, Dr. Ndalo, I'll give it a try."

"Okay…now tell me, you said you've finished your degree in journalism with a major in English?"

"Yes Sir, that's correct… I've been hunting for a job ever since, but I've not found anything yet… hopeful something will come my way soon… I'm tired of doing nothing."

"You've a very clear, bold and distinct voice... maybe you should try radio or television."

"I always dreamed of having my own radio show, since I was little. I used to grab my hair brush and pretend it was a radio microphone and make all my dolls listen to me."

"Hypothetically speaking, if you were given a slot on radio, what kind of a show would you like to have?"

"Healing hearts!" she said.

"Excuse me?" the doctor asked.

"I mean, I'll call the show 'Healing Hearts', and its main focus would be to stop people from making wrong decisions that could jeopardize their lives, especially women."

"Interesting... look Bonelwa, I would love to chat with you the whole day, but I have to attend a meeting... why don't you come see me on Monday morning at ten o'clock at our offices... and put your idea for the show on paper, it must be well detailed, okay?"

"I would love to, Dr. Ndalo, where are your offices?"

"Here is my other business card, all the information that you need is there."

Bonelwa took the card and read the details on it and said, "Are you the chairperson of FSH Media? That means you're in charge of all those radio stations across the country?"

"Yes, that's right, FSH Media, owns and operates ten radio stations across the country and one nationwide TV station."

"I'll be there on Monday morning, Dr. Ndalo, thank you!"

"Okay... I have to run now... I will see you on Monday."

The doctor paid the bill and left. Bonelwa's eyes watched the old man as he headed out of the coffee shop. She pulled out her phone, called Senzo and told him about her meeting with Dr. Ndalo.

On her way home, Bonelwa could not stop thinking about Dr. Ndalo's advice to reach out to her family.

After procrastinating and having a long conversation with herself, she finally decided to call her father.

"Hello," her father, Mavo, answered the call.

Bonelwa breathed heavily on the phone, she couldn't bring herself to speak.

"Hello," Mavo said, a bit irritated. He could hear the person breathing heavily on the phone.

"Hello… Hello…okay that's it, I'm hanging up," Mavo said, irritated.

"Dad…" Bonelwa finally said, tears rolling down her cheeks.

"Nelwa? Is that you, Nelwa?" Mavo asked, in tears.

"Yes, Dad… it's me."

"Thank God…" Mavo sighed deeply and asked, "Are you okay?"

"I'm fine, Dad."

"Thank God, you are fine… we've been worried sick all these years… we've looked for you everywhere, here and in Cape Town, but no one knew your whereabouts, we even reported you as a missing person," Mavo said, with tears of relieve.

"I'm so sorry, Dad… for disappearing on you guys like that…" Bonelwa burst into tears.

"It's okay, Sweetheart… it's okay… I'm just glad that you are fine," Mavo held his tears.

"Me too, Dad… is mom around?"

"Yes… Fezeka, Bongani, Abu… it's Nelwa!" Mavo shouted.

They all ran to the phone and took turns talking to her.

"Mom?" Bonelwa said.

"Yes, Honey... I'm right here," Fezeka wiped her tears.

"I want to come home..." Bonelwa said.

"Yes, Honey... please come home... I'll send you a flight ticket right away," Fezeka said.

"It's okay Mom, no need for that, thanks anyway," Bonelwa said, then asked her mother to give the phone to her dad. Mavo took the phone from Fezeka. Bonelwa told him about Senzo, Lwazi and their wedding plans, and said she would be coming with Senzo and Lwazi. Mavo told her that it was okay, she said goodbye and they both hung up.

That weekend, Bonelwa spent most of her time shaping up her idea for the show. Senzo helped her with ideas and views from the male perspective.

Monday morning at half past nine, Bonelwa arrived at the FSH Media office, and Dr. Ndalo was notified of her arrival. At ten o'clock someone came to fetch her from reception and led her to a board-room. When she entered the boardroom, she saw the board members of FSH Media, mostly old men and one old lady, all looking at her very seriously.

"Come on in, Ms. Hlazo... meet the board of FHS Media, they'll decide your fate. You have fifteen minutes to do your presentation," Dr. Ndalo said.

Bonelwa stood in front of the board and asked someone to help her connect her laptop to the projector, fixed her suit jacket, looked the board members in the eyes, and did what she does best. She articulately and effectively communicated to the board her vision for the show, backed it up with some hard facts, and made it visual with easy to understand graphics.

After her presentation, she gathered her belongings and was escorted out of the boardroom.

On Friday of that same week, Bonelwa was called back to FHS offices and was offered a three-year contract for a weekly afternoon slot for her show, which would be syndicated to all FHS owned radio stations across the country.

After reading the contract, she was happy with the terms and signed it. The contract stipulated that the first show would air within six months after the contract was signed. That gave her enough time to get married and prepare the topics for each show.

When she left FHS office, she called Senzo and gave him the good news. Senzo was extremely glad and suggested they go out to celebrate. The three of them went to a fancy restaurant and celebrated Bonelwa's new job.

The next weekend, Bonelwa, accompanied by Senzo and Lwazi, boarded the plane to Eastern Cape. After their arrival, on the way to Bonelwa's parents, in the taxi, Senzo, who was nervous throughout the trip, kept asking if he looked okay. Bonelwa assured him that he looked just fine.

When they arrived, they got out of the taxi. While the taxi driver was busy with their luggage, Senzo turned around to check his reflection in the taxi window. Bonelwa shook her head and said, "Would you relax? You're making me nervous!"

"Sorry... do you think your father will approve of me?"

"Yes..."

"Okay... how do I really look?"

Bonelwa moved closer to him, fixed his tie, looked him in the eye and said, "Perfect...you look just like the man of my dreams."

Senzo took a deep breath and said, "Okay...let's do this."

While he was still talking, Bonelwa's whole family came out of the house and headed toward them. Senzo paid the taxi driver and the taxi driver left.

Bonelwa's family was very excited to see her, they greeted each other, helped with their luggage and invited them inside.

Bongani and Abu showed Senzo the guestroom, while Bonelwa took Lwazi to her old room.

A few moments later, Senzo sat nervously in the living room, while he conversed with Mavo, Bongani and Abu. Fezeka, Bonelwa and Lwazi, joined them shortly.

After supper, Lwazi fell asleep, so Bonelwa took her to bed and then returned to the living room, where they all gathered. Senzo wanted to leave, to give Bonelwa some time to talk to her family, but Bonelwa asked him to stay. Bonelwa told her family everything that had happened to her, how she ended up in Johannesburg, and asked them to forgive her.

Upon hearing what had happened to her, the room became quiet. Everyone seemed sad and blamed themselves for not being there for her. Bonelwa sat there looking at their sad faces, felt guilty for disappearing on them without a trace. After a few moments of silence, they all agreed to forgive each other and put the past behind them.

The mood in the room shifted when Bonelwa changed the subject to her wedding, invited all of them, and asked her father to walk her down the aisle—her father could not have been happier. The weekend passed quickly and then Senzo, Bonelwa and Lwazi boarded a flight and returned to Johannesburg.

CHAPTER TWENTY-SIX

A t last, the day they had all been waiting for had arrived. Bonelwa wanted a private and intimate ceremony; and even though Senzo's parents wanted something extravagant, they respected Bonelwa's wish.

The venue was the garden at Senzo's grandfather's family residence.

Finally, after all the last minute final touch-ups, the hour for the proceedings had arrived. All was set, the groom was in his position, the groomsmen and bridesmaids were in their respective positions, then, the famous pianist hit the chords sounding the traditional bridal chorus, "Here Comes the Bride" and all were asked to rise. Bonelwa, accompanied by Mavo, marched along the red carpet to the gazebo.

Then the minister officiating the wedding asked all to sit. After everyone was seated, he began the ceremony with an introduction for the purpose of the gathering, "We are gathered here together in the sight of God, and in the presence of these witnesses to join Senzo and Bonelwa in the bonds of holy matrimony. If there is anyone here who knows a just cause why they should not lawfully be joined in marriage, I implore you to speak now, or forever hold your peace."

Senzo and Bonelwa anxiously held their breath in the silence that swept the garden after the question.

Since no one spoke against their marriage, the minister proceeded with the ceremony, "Who gives this woman to be married to this man?"

"I do," Mavo said.

Then looking at the couple, he said, "If it is of your own free will to take each other as husband and wife, please indicate such by joining your hands."

Senzo and Bonelwa joined their hands.

After reading a scripture from the Bible, and giving a brief sermon, he looked at Senzo and said, "Do you, Senzo Ntuli, take Bonelwa Amanda Hlazo to be your lawfully wedded wife, to love and to cherish, to have and to hold; and do you promise to love her and her alone, for as long as you both shall live?"

Senzo replied, "I do."

Then, looking at Bonelwa, the minister said, "Do you, Bonelwa Amanda Hlazo, take Senzo Ntuli to be your lawfully wedded husband, to love and to cherish, to have and to hold; and do you promise to love him and him alone, and to respect and obey him for as long as you both shall live?"

Bonelwa replied, "I do."

Then looking at Senzo again, he said, "Senzo, what would you like to give as a pledge to symbolize your love, sincerity and faithfulness to this woman?"

Senzo signalled his best man, and his best man reached into his inner pocket to get the ring, passed it to Senzo, and Senzo produced the ring as a symbol of his love.

Then the minister said to him, "Senzo, please repeat after me: 'This ring I give to you as a symbol of my love, sincerity, and faithfulness. Will you wear it as a symbol of your own love, sincerity, and faithfulness toward me?'"

Senzo carefully followed the minister, repeating every word. Bonelwa then responded, "I Will," and Senzo placed the ring on Bonelwa's finger. It was followed by emotional cheers by the hopelessly romantic among the guests.

Then the minister turned his gaze toward Bonelwa and said, "Bonelwa, what would you like to give, as a pledge, to symbolize your love, sincerity and faithfulness to this man?"

Khethiwe, Dr. Ndalo's youngest daughter, passed the ring to Bonelwa, and she produced the ring as a symbol of her love. Then the minister said to her, "Bonelwa, please repeat after me: 'This ring I give to you as a symbol of my love, sincerity, and faithfulness. Will you wear it as a symbol of your own love, sincerity, and faithfulness toward me?'"

Bonelwa repeated after the minister. Senzo then replied, "I Will," and Bonelwa placed the ring on Senzo's finger.

The minister proceeded by instructing Senzo to face Bonelwa, and hold her right hand with his right hand. With that done, he said, "Senzo, please repeat after me:

'I, Senzo Ntuli, take you, Bonelwa Amanda Hlazo, to be my wedded wife; to have and to hold from this day forward, for better or for worse, for richer or poorer, in sickness and in health, to love and to cherish, till death do us part, according to God's holy ordinance; I pledge to you my faithfulness.'"

Bonelwa watched Senzo's lips reciting those words and her mind took her back, reminding her of how far she had come, "What if somehow, he is also tempted by some beautiful and sexy girl? Will he be faithful to me or he will do to me what Tau has done to me?" That question distracted her and made her oblivious to what was going on in front of her.

"Bonelwa, please repeat after me…" the minister said. But noticing that she was in wonderland, the minister tried to bring her back to reality by whispering, "Bonelwa, are you okay? … Bonelwa?"

"Ahhn… yes, I'm fine, Sir, sorry about that. Please carry on."

"Bonelwa, please repeat after me: 'I, Bonelwa Amanda Hlazo, take you, Senzo Ntuli, to be my wedded husband; to have and to hold from this day forward, for better or for worse, for richer or poorer, in sickness and in health, to love, cherish, and to obey, till death do us part, according to God's holy ordinance; I pledge to you my faithfulness.'"

Then, looking at the audience, the minister announced: "Because Senzo and Bonelwa have consented together to be joined in holy matrimony, have declared it before God and these witnesses, and have thereto given and pledged their love and faithfulness to each other; by the power given to me by God and the law of this country, I pronounce them husband and wife, in the name of the Father, and of the Son, and of the Holy Spirit, Amen… Senzo, you may kiss the bride."

Senzo obeyed and kissed Bonelwa passionately for a good while, until the minister cleared his throat to signal that it was enough. They stopped kissing, feeling a bit embarrassed.

"Please turn around and face the guests," the minister requested with a half-smile. They both turned around and faced the guests.

"Ladies and Gentlemen, I give you, Mr. and Mrs. Ntuli!" the minister announced. His announcement was received with an eruption of celebration; and as the newlyweds marched along the red carpet, the guests threw violet petals at them.

While the bride and groom, along with their groomsmen, bridesmaids and family members took photos, the guests were entertained by a famous local band and drinks were served.

After speeches were made and other formalities were out of the way, the time came for the couple to open the dance floor for the eagerly awaiting guests.

As the sun set, Senzo and Bonelwa took to the well-kept grass as the live band played Sade's hit song, "By Your Side" Bonelwa's all-time favorite song. As the voice came out of the speakers, it was like Sade herself was singing, and Bonelwa got curious, looked at the stage, and it was indeed Sade! Senzo's mother had pulled some strings, and got Sade to surprise the couple, and sing her hit song, live and in person.

Bonelwa and Senzo were delighted by the generous surprise. Bonelwa leaned on Senzo's chest as they danced. She had some fears, but Senzo's heartbeat assured her that his heart was hers, and hers alone. Half way through the dance, Senzo gently pushed Bonelwa away to look into her eyes, and gave her a look that says, "Your heart is safe in my heart."

As the song was ending, others joined in, and Sade continued to delight the guests with her extraordinary voice, as she sang some of her all-time hit songs.

After dancing with her father, Mavo, Dr. Ndalo also asked Bonelwa for a dance, and while they danced, he said, "I was ready to be your dad not only for today, but also for the rest of my life."

Bonelwa leaned on his chest and said, "Thank you, Dad!"

Dr. Ndalo smiled and rejoiced at the sound of those words.

As the evening drew to an end, Senzo and Bonelwa left for the hotel, where they were to sleep, before they headed to Mauritius for their honeymoon.

The following day, they headed to the airport and took their flight to Mauritius. When they arrived at the sea-front hotel and checked in, the porter was told to take their luggage into their room.

Senzo took Bonelwa's hand and led her to the beach, where they took off their shoes and walked barefoot across the edges of the water. He stopped to see and hear the sound of the roaring waves, turned to Bonelwa, locked eyes with her and said, "I love you. I've never really stopped loving you, but for a while I learned to live without you… but right here, next to you, is where I truly belong."

Bonelwa eyed him with an intense desire to be in his arms. He picked her up and kissed her slowly, their lips locking and unlocking with an intense passion.

They returned to the hotel. When they got to the corridor, Senzo picked up Bonelwa into his arms and carried her to their room's door. Bonelwa opened the door and Senzo closed it with his heel. They spent most of their honeymoon in bed consummating their once lost love; making sure they nourish it each day with the water of their love.

CHAPTER TWENTY-SEVEN

Three months after their wedding, Bonelwa, who was now two months pregnant, started her work at the radio station.

On her very first show, after all the hype and advertisement, her producer signalled that she would be live in five seconds. As the countdown approached its end, she cleared her throat and nervously prepared her introductory lines.

"Welcome to Healing Hearts, a show where you're allowed to be yourself without fear of being judged. My name is Bonelwa Ntuli, and I will be your host. Thank you for tuning in, this is Loud FM 91.7, broadcasting from our studios in Johannesburg and syndicated across the country on all our sister radio stations... don't touch that dial, I'll be right back after this!"

Her voice faded to a quick jingle about the show. Her producer signalled her again to get ready in five seconds.

"Welcome back to Healing Hearts, a show where you're allowed to be yourself without fear of being judged. I'm your host, Bonelwa Ntuli.

"On this very first show, I would like to lay the foundation of the show with my own personal heart-breakings and walk of shame. Before I ask you to share your stories, let me go first, so that you can be confident in sharing your stories, without fear of being judged. So, here I go...

"I come from a very conservative family; the women on my mother's side of the family carry a very strong tradition which gave them a sense of purpose and dignity. My great-grandmother married as a virgin, my grandmother married as a virgin, my mother married as a virgin, and my older sister married as a virgin; and I too was made to promise to keep myself pure until I was married. And I kept that promise, until my second year in university. That was until I met my first love, a senior in his final year. After months of dating, I guess like most men, he wanted more than what I was giving him. I told him about my family tradition and the promise I'd made to my mother. He heard me and was fascinated by it, and I guess that made him want me even more. So, he countered my reasoning by making me another promise, which if he kept it, technically, would not affect my family tradition and the promise I made to my mother. So he said, 'I promise to marry you if you give yourself to me. Who would know whether you married a virgin or not, apart from you and me? Besides, what difference would a piece of paper, wedding clothing and celebration make? What we'll do that day in the bedroom is the same as we can do here and now. I swear, I'll marry you Baby, I promise.'

"His argument disarmed all my defences. He was the man I loved and wanted to spend the rest of my life with and I was not prepared to lose him. So I traded the promise I'd made to my mother, in exchange for his promise to marry me, and I gave myself to him that very night; and to be fair and honest, I wanted him as much he wanted me.

"After that, all was well and he kept his eyes and love on me only, reassuring me almost daily that he was a man of his word, and that he would marry me. He was sincere in his promise, and what calmed my fears, was that he always kept the promises he made to me.

"A few months later, I went home for a holiday, and was expecting my phone to be flooded with his text messages of love, as he always did… but I was in for a rude awakening… there were no messages for me, even after I texted him several times. Eventually, when I decided to call him, his phone was off… and to cut a long story short, I cut my holiday short and rushed back to the campus, only to find out that he was seduced by my best friend and the two of them were somehow in love. She got pregnant, he married her, and did not keep the promise he had made me. That devastated me. I was suffocating inside and had to tell someone… so, I told my mother and she was very disappointed… my father looked at me as though somehow I was dirty, and he didn't talk to me much after that. The worst part was that my family tradition was well known in our area and some neighbours could not wait for the day that they could throw some mud into my parents' faces. I gave them that privilege when the rumours from the university reached my neighbourhood and caused everyone to gossip about my parents. My parents walked in shame with their heads down…

"I left home that day and I had not returned until recently… I had to face my youthful battles on my own and that caused me to make many more mistakes along the way.

"The worst decision I made, was to avenge myself on the ones who had hurt me. I did many terrible things to try to make him jealous and show him what he had lost; to make him feel the pain I was feeling inside…"

She continued to tell the audience all she'd gone through in life and ended by saying, "I thought that by dating other people in front of him, I would hurt him. I didn't just want to hurt him, but also any other men that would come my way. I didn't care, because of my pain. But the truth is, the only one I was hurting was me. I put my whole life on hold to dedicate myself to proving to him that I was worthy to be loved. In pursuing that path, I almost destroyed my life! But I thank God, that in the midst of my pain and hopelessness, He sent, once again into my path, a man who loves me more than I love myself. A man that loved me when I could not love myself. His love disarmed all my fears, mended my heart and made it whole again. He put a ring on my finger and today I'm carrying his child, made in love.

"Now, before I open the lines to hear your stories, I want to encourage all our listeners who are going through a rough patch right now... cease to avenge yourself, the only one that will actually get hurt, is you! Please remember, it's not over yet... love may just surprise you when you least expect it... I'll be right back to take your calls after this!"

After the commercials, she returned and said, "Welcome back to Healing Hearts, a show where you're allowed to be yourself, without fear of being judged. I'm your host, Bonelwa Ntuli. We have a caller on the line. Hello, Caller, what's your story?"

"I'm so sorry, Nelwa..."

"Mom?"

"I want to say this in public...please forgive me for deserting you in your time of distress," her mother said, in tears.

"I've have forgiven you, Mom. I'm so sorry for breaking the family tradition, and the promise I'd made to you. Please forgive me."

"I've forgiven you, Honey... oh my baby..."

"Mom, even though I've failed, I want you to know that I respect and honour our noble family tradition. I'll pass it on to my daughters and guide them to keep it in the family."

"Oh… Honey… I just thank God you're well! tomorrow, I'm coming to see you in Johannesburg."

"Okay Mom, thank you, I'll see you tomorrow."

"Bye, Honey"

"Bye, Mom," she said and played a jingle to give her mother her details off-air. She returned on air saying, "Wow! That was an unexpected call from my mom. We're still taking calls, and we have another caller. Hello, Caller, what's your story?"

"Hi, Bonelwa, I just want to thank you. You've saved me from making a big mistake… I was actually on my way to my ex-boyfriend's best friend's, to have revenge sex with him, to get back at my boyfriend for cheating on me; but after hearing your story, I couldn't go through with it. I turned around and drove back home, so thank you, keep up the good work you're doing, bye!"

"Wow! I'm glad to hear that I could help, thank you for sharing, Anonymous! We have another caller… Hello, welcome to Healing Hearts… what's your story?"

"Hi, Bonelwa, thank you for sharing your story. My name is Getty, I'm currently in a relationship with one of my baby's daddy's co-workers, just to get back at him. But, the truth is, I don't love the guy and he knows it and plays along with it. The stupid thing is that while I think I'm using him, he's the one using me for sex. I'm terminating the relationship, if I can call it that, right away! Thank you!"

"Thank you for sharing, Getty! We have another caller on the line… Hello, Caller?"

"Hi, Bonelwa, my name is Tony. I've recently cheated on my girl-friend with her best friend, and it hurt her so badly that she wants to sleep with all my friends just to get back at me. I just hope she's listening, I don't want her to get any more hurt than I already hurt her, thanks."

"Thank you for sharing, Tony. I hope you've learned your lesson."

Listeners continued to call and share their stories on air.

The show continued to grow and the ratings of the show spiked rocket-high as more and more people tuned in to Bonelwa's show. It became very popular and she was even offered a TV talk show.

Two months later, around midnight, Bonelwa could not sleep. She got up from the bed, went to the study room, opened her laptop and wrote the last chapter of her memoir. Finally typing "The End" with a big smile of satisfaction on her face.

Five months later, Bonelwa was rushed to the hospital and gave birth to a baby boy. When she awoke, she found Senzo and Lwazi looking at her with amazement. She greeted them, asked Lwazi to come sit next to her, and asked the nurse to bring the baby.

The nurse brought in the baby and placed him in Bonelwa's arms. Lwazi could not wait to get a glimpse at her baby brother. Bonelwa uncovered his face for Lwazi to see and Lwazi looked at him with great amazement.

Senzo sat on the other side of the bed, and asked them to smile, as he took a selfie of him and his family.

Bonelwa held her baby with great joy in her heart; it was all she'd ever wanted—a family with a man that loved and adored her.

~*~ The End ~*~

Dear reader, thank you for taking the time to read this book, I really appreciate.

I hope you have enjoyed reading this book.

If you have any suggestions, comments or questions regarding a character, the story or anything concerning this book, or if you just want to say hi, you can reach me on my personal email: **ramostalaya@gmail.com**

Readers have the power to make or break a book through reviews and recommending it to others. If you were touched and you've enjoyed this book, please consider leaving a review on Amazon, iBooks, Kobo, Facebook and Goodreads, even if it's just a short review; it would make all the difference and would be very much appreciated.

If you would like to receive an email when Ramos's next book is released, please visit: **http://eepurl.com/-Mbnz** . You will only be contacted when a new book is released, your email address will never be shared, and you can unsubscribe at any time. Thank you for your support.

www.ingramcontent.com/pod-product-compliance
Lightning Source LLC
Chambersburg PA
CBHW020319200626
46814CB00006BA/2324